THE CHAPLAINS
Trilogy

Moles in the Eagle's Nest

Army Chaplain Eric Lovejoy stumbles onto a secret organization that is trying to narrow the gap between the earnings of corporate executives and their workers.

Tainted Hero

Army Hospital Chaplain David Huffnor finds himself in the dangerous position of trying to rescue a former WAC who is trapped in a life she didn't expect.

A SHIPWRECK SURVIVOR'S TALE: Letters to His Grandchildren

Retired Army chaplain Gregg Sponney, stranded on an uninhabited island, details his adventure and shares his views on what is important in life.

A SHIPWRECK SURVIVOR'S TALE:
LETTERS TO HIS GRANDCHILDREN

THE CHAPLAINS
BOOK 3

DONALD G. VEDELER

iUniverse, Inc.
NEW YORK   BLOOMINGTON

A SHIPWRECK SURVIVOR'S TALE:
Letters to His Grandchildren

iUniverse books may be ordered through booksellers or by contacting:

iUniverse
1663 Liberty Drive
Bloomington, IN 47403
www.iuniverse.com
1-800-Authors (1-800-288-4677)

Because of the dynamic nature of the Internet, any Web addresses or links contained in this book may have changed since publication and may no longer be valid. The views expressed in this work are solely those of the author and do not necessarily reflect the views of the publisher, and the publisher hereby disclaims any responsibility for them.

ISBN: 978-1-4401-7648-7 (sc)
ISBN: 978-1-4401-7649-4 (ebk)

Printed in the United States of America

iUniverse rev. date: 10/1/2009

DEDICATION

To everyone who has ever been a grandchild or a grandparent.
To my three grandchildren: Katharine, Andrew and Christopher.

PROLOGUE

On Monday, June 19th, 2006, a violent Pacific Ocean storm surprised West Coast meteorologists.

Born of an unusual confluence of warmer than usual mid-Pacific waters, a huge area of moisture-laden air, a westerly variation in the jet stream, and the pull of a low pressure area, what might have been simply another ocean storm, became a "perfect summer storm."

It raced to the northwest, generating winds of near hurricane force, and creating fifty foot waves. Ocean going ships, warned by urgent radio messages, fled east and west of its path at full speed. Some stayed on course and rode out the storm with minor damage.

By Wednesday, June 30th, the depression had battered the Near Islands and Rat Islands of the Aleutian Island chain, and swept into the Bering Sea between Alaska and Russia. In early July, by the time it had traveled another three hundred miles to Pribilot Island, a little over two hundred miles west southwest of Alaska's Nunivak Island and Hooper Bay, it had degenerated into a wide-spread cluster of rain squalls among patches of blue sky. It would later die as a rainy, windy area of whitecaps pushed by twenty to thirty knot winds, with ragged clouds showing broad patches of blue sky. A few days later, the Bering Strait weather radar showed nothing.

The storm had minimal effect on northern Pacific shipping, but was of gigantic significance for fifteen passengers and five crewmembers aboard a wooden, 72 foot, Sparkman & Stephens Yawl on its way from Alaska to Japan.

Caught, after midnight, by a violent wind sheer early in the storm, with only one reef in the mainsail, the old vessel was dismasted. When the mainmast went over the side, it carried the small aft mast with it. Dragged alongside, the masts crashed against the hull with every wave. Frantic crewmembers chopped away at the stays, and after a wild struggle, the entire mess sank, freeing the sailboat from the relentless pounding. Three hours later a rogue wave, twice the size of those already generated by the growing storm, rolled the buttoned-up yawl, severely injuring several passengers, and washing one crewmember away, safety harness and tether included. The engine, partially torn from its anchor bolts by the rollover, died. The heavy keel brought the vessel upright and it wallowed wildly and helplessly, further injuring those aboard.

LETTERS TO HIS GRANDCHILDREN

Dear Family,

This will be a short, preliminary note.

We have been shipwrecked on a rocky island! Five days ago! Three of us survived: Harry O'Toole, Melanie Pickett, and me. We are bruised and battered, cold, and wet. I will write more later, but for now I want to briefly record what we have been struggling with these past few days.

We have limped about gathering anything we could find from our wrecked sailing ship, surviving on four loaves of bread, tied in a white trash bag, that somehow floated ashore intact, and a large, half empty plastic jar of peanut butter. We drink water from the many pools of rainwater in rock hollows.

Harry had a dislocated shoulder, which Melanie "reduced" as she called it; she then made a temporary sling for his arm, using a shirt taken from a dead shipmate. Our sprains and bruises impede our work, but we feel we must cobble together a primitive shelter from the chilly wind, rain showers, and fog. Melanie has a sprained wrist, which we have wrapped and splinted as best we can.

Today we struggled in the lee of a four foot tall boulder to make a simple lean-to out of driftwood. Although it only provides minimal protection, it gets us out of the worst of the wind and some of the rain.

This is a personal tragedy beyond imagining. We are cold, in shock, and scared.

I am able to write this note because a footlocker from our boat washed up on the rocky shore! Believe it or not, it had pens and lined pads of paper in it! We spotted it bobbing in a somewhat sheltered inlet, if you could call a gap in the boulders where the surf ran in with a little less violence than elsewhere, "an inlet!" It's almost as though God delivered the footlocker in Person, as though He knew we would need to do something to repair our devastated morale. It was Melanie who suggested we can now write letters, which seems kind of like an exercise in futility. Not much else we can do today.

More later, but rest and sleep are a must.

Love to all of you, my dear ones! Grampa Gregg

Dear Family,

Since Monday we have calmed down some, along with the weather, and we are trying to take stock of our very perilous predicament. After a thorough exploration we know that we are alone on this island, and can find no evidence that anyone has ever set foot on it.

I have decided to address any letters that may follow this one to our grandchildren. This is also addressed to you, my dear wife Ella, and to our own grown children, Matt, Beth, & Gloria, and, of course their spouses, Susan, Ed, and Clyde. Although I am writing to your children; I must assume that all of you will be reading whatever I write.

Dear Heidi, Edward, Billy, Katie, Chris, Helga, and Andy,

I am writing especially to you, mainly because I have spent so little time with each of you. I wish, now that I can do nothing about it, that it had been more.

Of course, there is the larger concern: I don't know if you'll ever get these letters. How long will we be stranded here? A month? A year? Forever? Regardless of how long we may be stuck here, there is much I want to share with you, things I wish I had managed to share back when it would have been possible to do so. Most importantly: I love you more than my words can ever express. You are my grandchildren, my very special grandchildren. I've loved every minute spent with each of you, watching you learn and grow and enjoy life. I hope I will see you again, but that is iffy, at best. I know I have not been the best grandfather I could be, but that has nothing to do with how much I love you all, and how I wish I could be around to make it up to you.

As you have learned by reading this, assuming you ever get it, we were shipwrecked on the shores of this small, uninhabited speck of land, in the middle of who-knows-where.

It has been seven days since we were thrown onto this island. We have more or less recovered from our injuries, so I will try to recount what happened and describe our situation.

Here are the details about our group: We "Adventure Tourists" were on our way from Juneau, after four days of hiking, culminating with our daylong hike on the Mendenhall Glacier. Then we were to go on to Japan's Hokkaido Island, which is north of Honshu, the main island of Japan. There we were to be driven to Daisetsuzan National Park to do some hiking. We were to camp out for four days in tents provided by the park service there. After Hokkaido we were to continue on to New Zealand, where, as prearranged, I was to depart for home. The *Windsong II* was a 72 foot Sparkman & Stephens Yawl, built in 1938. It had been practically rebuilt and also reconfigured below decks to accommodate fifteen passengers and five crewmembers. It would then continue on to Tahiti, and then to South America, carrying my replacement guest.

2

Adventure Tours runs a year long trip at $12,000 per month. I could not afford the whole trip, and besides, I wanted to come home after the first four months of "adventure."

This was to have been my "big fling," a chance to do something active while I was still young enough and fit enough to do so. Next year Ella and I were going on a string of Elderhostel travel programs as our "big fling" together. Now? Well, at this point, I don't know what my future holds.

Here's what happened to land us in the precarious situation: On June 21st, late in the afternoon, dark clouds appeared to our south. The captain assured us that we could handle a summer storm at sea, so we "buttoned up" the boat. We were told to put the last of our toiletries and personal items into our sea bags (large waterproof duffle bags in which we kept anything we were not using at the moment) and seal them tight. We then climbed into our bunks, strapped ourselves in and hung on as the boat rocked and corkscrewed in increasingly larger waves.

Sometime after midnight, what the crew described as a "wind sheer" tore both of our masts away. We were stunned by the mind boggling violence and noise when this happened. The crew fought desperately to get rid of the tangled mess hanging over the side, banging loudly against the hull. Using bolt cutters and a small ax they chopped at the stays. The bolt cutters were lost overboard when a heavy wave slapped the man using them, washing him over the rail, where he hung by his safety harness, until he could be pulled back aboard.

Over the next few hours, when we ventured to the cockpit hatch to take a look, we were blasted by powerful winds, stung by driving, horizontal rain, and thrown about by huge waves. On the third night of the storm, a huge "rogue wave", as the crew called it, rolled us completely over in the early morning darkness. We lost one crewman in that instant, with no possible way of turning and going back to look for him. When the boat righted itself, thanks to the heavy, deep keel, and the fact that we were securely buttoned up, we found that we were all bruised and battered even more than before!

Not much later, a crewmember shouted above the storm noise to tell us that the motor had somehow been damaged, and had quit. So we were without its steadying influence. It is essential to keep the bow of a boat pointed into the waves during bad weather. The bow breaks up the waves and usually allows the boat to ride up and over them, thus providing the best chance of remaining afloat. Without power or steerage way, *Windsong II* was helplessly tossed about with ever more violent motion. The crew struggled in the raging seas to deploy our sea anchor, a cone shaped, heavy duty canvas "bag" with a large hole at the bottom. Once it was tied to the forward bow cleat, it more or less kept our bow pointed upwind into the monstrous waves. Without its steadying influence we would have remained sideways to the waves and most certainly would have been rolled repeatedly.

Two fellow travelers suffered severe head injuries as they were thrown about inside the main cabin when we rolled. We struggled to return the injured to their bunks and strap them in as securely as we could. Two others suffered broken arms, and many of us bore sprained wrists and ankles.

The next morning, after the rollover, water in the bilges rose to the cabin floor, so those of us who were not too badly injured were set to work bailing, passing buckets and dish pans of water to the crewman in the half open hatch. Another crewmember was eventually able to find the leak and slow the inflow of water somewhat.

We were battered by heavy seas, wallowing helplessly for days on end as the winds pushed us off, to somewhere, we knew not where. Those of us who were not strapped into our bunks were tossed about helplessly, and injuries mounted with every passing hour. One of the passengers died at some point during all this; we just left him lashed in his bunk.

And then it happened: As the murky sky grew darker with the approach of yet another dreaded night, after a brutal week of wild, storm tossed days, exhausted and frightened, we gradually became aware of the roaring and deep booming of heavy surf. Blinded by torrential rain, wind driven yellow sea foam, near total darkness, and roiling seas, we sensed our vessel nearing an unknown shore. We were told to gather our individual sea bags and throw them overboard, in the hope that some of us and some of them would wash ashore. Shortly thereafter, a huge wave peaked and roared down on us. The line holding the sea anchor parted and we lost it! The *Windsong II* rapidly turned sideways to the waves. This was a disastrous turn of events that made what happened next worse, if that is possible. In heavy surf, sometime around midnight, amid increasingly confused and gigantic waves, we crashed sideways onto the boulder strewn shore of this rocky island. Accompanied by violent, roaring confusion, our boat broke apart and we were thrown into the surf, on a wild and rocky shore.

Sometime later, I don't know how much later, I slowly regained my senses and found myself lying between two rocks on shore, the lower half of my body being repeatedly washed over by the icy remnants of foaming waves. In the faint light, I squinted against the rain and watched as pieces of our wooden vessel were lifted and hurled again and again on the rocks with thunderous cracks and booms. I caught glimpses of huge sections of hull and deck rising atop mountainous waves and being dashed on the rocks. Several times I saw them break into smaller pieces amid the unrelenting fury of the huge waves.

As a welcome twilight ushered in the dawn, three of us survivors found each other and dragged our battered bodies along the shore, searching for other survivors.

As I already mentioned, there were twenty of us aboard: five crewmembers, and we fifteen "Adventure Tourists." Four were dead by the time the wild surf threw them up on the rocky shore. Two died within hours of being smashed by the surf onto the rocks. Three bodies came ashore during our first two days. The three of us who survived were battered and injured to some degree

Well, dear ones, we are running out of daylight; can't see to keep writing. So I will end today's letter and continue our tale tomorrow. I love you!

Love, Grampa

DAY 8
THURSDAY, JULY 6ᵀᴴ, 2006

Dear Grandchildren,

The sun has peeked through the fast moving clouds. We found enough driftwood, and a large number of two-by-fours to improve our primitive lean-to shelter in the lee of a large boulder. Apparently some ship lost a packet of lumber overboard, probably in a storm. Because it is so very windy here, we need to strengthen our shelter, by rolling stones against the driftwood supports. With a couple of rain suits from our deceased fellow travelers woven into the sloping roof, we were able to make it ever so slightly water repellant, although we could not possibly stay dry in it during any rain. We wear our storm gear, even when we are inside our pathetic little shelter.

Today, we also managed to make a few brief attempts at retrieving things from the wreck of our once beautiful yacht. There is a lot of debris from our vessel scattered all along the shore, much of it under water. And the water is very, very cold. We found three small tins of biscuits, two plastic bags, each with two loaves of bread, another large half empty plastic tub of peanut butter. Fortunately, enough of the peanut butter had been used so that the container floated! We also found a Boston Red Sox baseball cap, and a cracked oar from the dinghy. A lot of good that will do! Not much to survive on, but at this point we are too beat up to do much poking around in the icy water.

Although I may never see any of you again, I would like to share what weighs on my heart today. Despair. We are pretty much bereft of hope. In fact, we are struggling with the grief process. And it is a difficult process: denial, loss of hope, and a feeling that life has lost its meaning. Later hope will come, and a fresh start. At least I hope so. I have observed and empathized with many a parishioner who has experienced loss — a loved one, a job, a home, a friendship, a pet — the list of life's losses is extensive. I will deal with my grief as best I can.

What to do? I will step back and try to focus on the bright side, admit my anger about what has happened to me, let myself cry. I will ask God to give me inner strength to fortify my resolve and carry on in spite of this bad thing that has happened. I will be sympathetic toward Harry and Melanie, not just what they are going through inside themselves, but I'll also try to set an example of courage and optimism.

And you, dear ones? You will have to face loss and grief at times. Maybe you already have. What can you do about it? Recognize that there is such a thing as "good grief." Good grief heals. It is a normal part of life, or can be. Expect it. You can ask God to help you, inwardly, to deal with your pain and to move on with your life in spite of it.

Daylight is fading fast; I can't see what I'm writing. So, more later.

Love, Grampa

5

Dear Grandchildren,

This morning, a very windy rain storm blew in from our west. The winds, we estimate, gusted around sixty or seventy miles per hour! Result? Our shelter, such as it was, blew apart and the pieces were scatted over an area one hundred yards long! As quickly as it arrived, the storm ended.

So we spent the late afternoon rebuilding, trying to make it stronger by dragging and rolling more, and bigger, rocks against the bases of the driftwood tree parts that made up the lean-to. We have managed to strip two more ponchos and rain pants from the dead and have tied arms and legs of the waterproof material together to improve the leaky roof.

I forgot one thing in my letter yesterday. Actually I probably have forgotten a lot of things. I do not ask God to rescue us. You may well ask, why not? The answer is simple: what if months go by and there is no rescue? Do I get mad at God? Do I accuse Him of being coldhearted and uncaring? Or, do I accept life's randomness and unpredictability, and seek solace and wisdom from within? As the old saying goes, "God is Spirit and they that worship Him must worship Him in spirit and in truth." For the word "worship" substitute the words "deal with." The message is clear. Well, it is to me anyhow. Do not blame God when things go wrong. What do you gain by doing so? Only bitterness. If someone is cured of a terrible disease, and I am not, is it not foolish to blame God? I vote for choice number two: seek God's inner presence to "see you through" whatever happens in life.

There is a fundamental issue here, one that I hope you will someday be able to resolve. It's this: is God an indwelling Reality or is He a busy guy who runs around <u>doing</u> things, like making earthquakes, causing accidents, and saving some to live longer while letting others die? Substitute "kills others" for the words "letting others die." At issue here is the question of free will. How free would we be to learn and grow if God did all the work for us? Life lays constant choices at our feet. Choice is something that goes on inside us, where, I believe, God is present and available.

Afterthought: what possible purpose is served by being angry at God? Will our anger change God's mind? Of course not! So let go of the notion of "God, the Manipulator," who kills and wounds some of us, yet heals and repairs others. I, for one, cannot worship, praise, nor love such an arbitrary God.

So there you have, in a nutshell, how I am trying to deal with being shipwrecked on a remote island, and with losing seventeen friends/acquaintances so abruptly and violently.

Too tired to write more.

Love, Grampa

Dear Grandchildren.

You won't believe this: Early this morning, before daylight, another huge wind knocked our shelter to pieces again. No wind or rain this time, just patches of fast moving fog! What a rude awakening!

After the air had been turned blue by our angry cursing, Harry shook his head and with a rueful grin on his face, commented, "I think we may need a course in Anger Management!"

That relaxed things enough so that we could begin to consider rebuilding our lean-to, again!

But we may have a solution: During our exploring we found a rocky gully nearby, maybe eight feet wide and six feet deep. It is only about ten feet long, but is quite deep in the middle. We have gathered a lot of driftwood, and are starting to build a new shelter, in the gully.

Harry noticed that runoff water from yesterday's rain was flowing down the bottom of the channel, which has a foot deep, narrow V at the bottom of the gully. So we wrestled stones across it and bridged the water, more or less, using rocks to form a fairly level floor. We hope the tunnel under our stone floor will be able to carry any runoff from future rains. We don't want to be sleeping in a brook!

With Harry's expertise, we jammed driftwood across and against both sides of the ditch and erected a cozy shelter. It measured something like four feet by eight feet at the stone floor level. We piled rocks against every part we could, wrapped the whole thing in ponchos and clothes taken from our dead fellow travelers, and jammed more branches and rocks against the whole thing. We cannot stand upright inside, but we are sheltered and sort of dry, and that's important.

We think, hope, and pray, that our new shelter will withstand the next wind storm. It seems very sturdy. We have pushed and shoved against it and it does not budge!

We have gathered a considerable hoard of clothes and food. We were able to gather foodstuffs from the shore where it all washed into shallows where we were able to reach it. Everything we own is crammed into and around our "gully house." God help us if heavy rains rise above our stone bridge floor!

Tomorrow we will work some more to strengthen our "home away from home."

I should comment here about our physical condition. One of the requirements for taking part in Adventure Tours was that we must be in good physical condition, able to hike, and climb for extended periods of time. I don't know how we could have done all the moving and lifting of rocks and large branches if we were not in good shape. What about your physical condition? Are you getting plenty of exercise, walking, running, for heart and lung health, lifting weights for strength? I hope you are, for you never know what demands may be put on your body. Plus you can do more and recover more quickly when you are fit. If you are not doing so now, I strongly urge you to begin! Use those muscles. Condition those lungs. Exercise that heart muscle.

"Anger Management." Hmmm. Maybe I should write a little about that to you. What is anger? And how might we manage it? First of all we need to consider the source of it. I am convinced that ninety percent of our anger arises as a reaction to being hurt. By "hurt" I mean disappointed in someone's behavior toward us, being ridiculed, insulted, laughed at. You know, the kinds of things that hurt our feelings in one way or another. So we get mad and sulk, or lash out in retaliation. This morning I got angry with God and wanted to yell at Him, "Why did you do that? What possible purpose could there be in your knocking down our shelter again?" Then sanity struck and I realized two things. One, I don't believe God has any interest in micro-managing our physical existence on Earth. And, two, storming around in a fury swearing and kicking things serves no useful purpose. Better to use that anger energy, emerging out of hurt, in a more practical manner and get busy rebuilding. Some people would collapse to the ground, and sit there in a state of depression. I personally think depression is a state of repressed anger.

We can best manage anger by first acknowledging that it stems from "hurt". So, if I am offended, hurt, or disappointed, what to do about it? Lash out and make the world a more wounded and angry place? Or seek some means of reconciliation with the person or event that hurt us? Duh! Better to talk calmly and rationally with someone than to seek to hurt them in return. And when life gives you a challenge, rise to it. Find a way to walk away from the situation or a way to try to fix it. Maybe you need to get away from the event and calm down. That's what all that stuff about "counting to ten" is about. Some people and events are best dealt with by abandoning them, by walking away, by doing something else, being somewhere else, thinking about something else. Often the source of our anger, and the anger itself, simply dissipates and we can get on with our lives unscathed by it.

The worst way to manage anger is to let it burst into flame and use it to lash out at the cause of it. So, stay calm, walk away, and think about the matter. Evaluate your alternatives and make a smart choice.

I know you have been angry at your friends at times; I was there with a couple of you at those times. I wonder how you dealt with it when you saw those friends next. Whether or not you did the wise thing then, maybe you will next time.

I miss you all so very much!

Love, Grampa

Good morning, Grandchildren!

I don't mean to trivialize our situation by sounding cheery and happy-go-lucky, but wallowing in despair is not healthy, and it is not my style. If I could survive Vietnam's horror, and still keep my sense of humor, then I can handle this!

So there are just the three of us, two weeks after being shipwrecked. Three survivors: Melanie Pickett, a 67 year old, tall and slender retired emergency room nurse; Harry O'Toole, a 70 year old, retired carpenter (funny name for a carpenter, eh? O'Toole?). He's a short muscular fellow with a body like a fireplug. And then there's me, your, 62 year old, retired Army Chaplain Grandfather. Information for our finders: my name is Gregg Sponney. I grin as I read what I have written so far in my first five letters. Not exactly the kind of adventure we signed on for, is it?

We have been here for two weeks. Slowly our cuts and bruises have healed, and we are relieved to discover that our bones and joints are returning to good working order. Melanie's left wrist is still wrapped and hangs in a sling; but we don't think anything is broken. My bruised ribs are less painful when I move and I can take deeper breaths now. Harry's apparently broken nose is getting better and his two black eyes are improving. The black and blue bruising is changing to yellow and green. Pretty soon we will stop calling him "Raccoon!" His dislocated shoulder seems almost as good as new. This is beginning to feel like some sort of Robinson Crusoe adventure, which we would gladly do without!

I must, with heavy heart, tell you about our first day. During that first wild night we dragged our six unfortunate companions into the lee of a large boulder, safely above the waves. It was only after the nine of us were huddled together that we came to realize that four of them were dead. The other two were semiconscious and very severely injured. As I already mentioned, in the July 5th letter, they died within hours. We three survivors were far too exhausted and disoriented to do anything further, so we huddled together and dozed off and on until sometime that first morning. Reluctantly we stripped the six dead, five men and one woman, deciding that their clothes, life vests and rain gear would most likely become necessary parts of our survival. More disheartening still was the finding of three more dead friends down the shore a few hundred yards to the east of us. We buried all of them as best we could.

Anyhow, here are the essentials: We have trudged along the entire southern coast of our island collecting what we could that might be useful for survival. In the first two days Harry and I were able to gather many pieces of our boat, some driftwood, a dozen partially damaged two-by-fours, and several empty plastic, gallon size water bottles. Now, with our sturdy gully shelter, we feel a bit more secure. It's not much, but for us, it is "Home Sweet Home."

We also managed to wade and swim to parts of the wreckage and collect a large quantity of canned goods, bottles of water, and a few other items, including the boat's first aid kit. During the storm, at the request of our skipper, we were all wearing as much clothing as we could, then on top of that our life vests, and over all of it, our rain gear. Everything was soaked, but the many layers acted rather like wet suits, so we are able to stand the frigid water and the cold, damp air. The water is so frigid that we cannot remain in it for more than a few minutes at a time. We collected things that washed ashore, or close to shore in shallow water, including the footlocker, which I mentioned in an earlier letter, which we found on our fifth day here. It had a strange conglomeration of contents: six unopened plastic wrapped packages of pads of lined, white, letter sized paper. We were encouraged to keep journals of our "adventure." They were to be collected when we returned to Adventure Tours' home base, where a secretary would type them up, and each individual's pages bound in a colorful binder, and then sent to us as a Memory Book. We also retrieved four six packs of ballpoint pens, four lightweight summer blankets, three dozen pair of white athletic socks, a dozen T-shirts and boxer shorts, a nylon windbreaker, a yellow poncho, three old copies of Golf Digest, a soggy 2006 calendar, a fourteen-inch Sword Demon knife with a saw-back blade, and several packs of flashlight batteries. Of course there was no flashlight anywhere, so the batteries are useless. Scattered among the rocks and tidal pools we found several loaves of shrink-wrapped stale bread, and the usual black plastic wrapped food items: boxes of crackers and cereal, bags of dried fruit and trail mix. This would be enough edibles to sustain us for a month or two, if we were to limit what we consume.

Three days ago as Melanie was walking along the shore some distance from our shelter, she made a wonderful find: a large, dented and scratched metal case that held a Sterno stove, three Butane lighters, and eight six packs of fuel cans!

We have done the best we could at remembering the names of our dead comrades, and where they were from. Melanie, who has an amazing memory for details, has written everything down on a sheet of the lined paper. I trust that, by the time you are reading this, the information has been sent to whatever authorities will need the information to contact next of kin.

Trouble is, we have no idea where we are. We had left Alaska and were headed in a southwesterly direction, heading for northern Japan. Oh, yes, you already know this! I see that I ramble. Must be the delayed shock of being stranded here? Also, I stop writing from time to time to think, to talk with Melanie and Harry, or to go drag some wood to our "campsite." So I sometimes forget what I've already written.

Nor do we have any notion of when we will be missed or how anyone would know where to begin a search for us. The last radio transmission from our boat was that late afternoon when we saw the dark clouds approaching and thought we might be in for "a little weather," as the captain put it. Hah! Little did we know then what fate had in store for us!

If we are never rescued, it is irrelevant to write that the island is about a mile long and maybe half mile wide. It is shaped like the steeply rounded back of a turtle with a fairly steep, rocky cliff east of our shelter. The cliff makes up about one fourth of the side on which we first arrived. It turns out, that after the sun finally broke through, we were able to figure that our side of the island faces roughly south west. The rocky ground is thick with grasses, small shrubs, and hundreds of seagulls! And rocks: boulders as big as houses, and as small as gravel size pebbles. There is some sand between the rocks on shore on the far side of the island, even a few stretches of sandy beaches, on that more sheltered downwind side. Above the high tide line on the "beach side" of our island, there is a lot of tall grass, with small heads of seed pods, which look like some sort of grain, Behind our shelter, up on the flat area is a shallow, boggy depression a couple of hundred yards across, where some larger shrubs and small stunted trees struggle to live. Areas of small shrubs and tall grasses are growing in and around the depression, in fairly good looking soil, especially where the gulls have fertilized it.

We guess the highest point on the island is a hundred feet above sea level. Our crevasse shelter is some 30 feet above the high tide line. We think (hope?) that will protect us from future storm waves.

There is a two foot wide crack in the rocky shore about fifty yards west of our shelter. At high tide the surf sloshes up the crack and carries away anything loose in it. So…? We have an automatic flush toilet that cleans itself out twice a day! Harry rigged a log across the top for a toilet seat, not very comfortable but very practical.

That pretty much describes the place. If we are found, you will be able to get all the details of our "Island Home Away from Home" from our finders, or, hopefully, from us. Maybe someday I'll sketch a map.

There are thousands of noisy sea birds everywhere. We see many nests with eggs, a hopeful sign for our survival. Melanie found a piece of fish net, about ten feet square, jammed in a large, eight foot section of the bow. We might somehow be able to use it to catch fish and seabirds. We'll see about that. Oh, yes, and there are seals. Lots of seals are gathered near one end of the island.

It seems to be quite rainy here. We are collecting water in the plastic bottles, by letting it run off our shelter and the slickers that cover most of the roof. There are many puddles in low spots and in depressions in some of the boulders. But then, there are the seagulls, for whom the whole island is a toilet, including the puddles. We have taken a few short "test drinks" from the water flowing under the floor of our shelter. So far, no ill effects from that. When the sun comes out we warm ourselves and dry our gear. But most days it is quite chilly here, maybe 50 to 60°, even though it's July. We worry about what winter might bring.

We have not seen any boats during our two weeks here. But fog has limited the visibility most of the time. So we still don't know if fishing boats pass anywhere near our island.

Love, Grampa

Dear Grandchildren,

As you can imagine, Harry, Melanie, and I have had a lot of time to talk during these first nineteen days here. If we are here for very long we will know all there is to know about each other, that's for sure.

We spend several hours each day collecting driftwood and looking for edible plants. This afternoon, after a skimpy lunch of the last of the stale, somewhat moldy bread, with peanut butter, we sat ourselves down to write letters. I have already written six letters, as I hope you will find out someday. So we are writing now, in the middle of a cloudy, drizzly afternoon, crowded together on the floor of our shelter. It is quite dark in here, but there is enough light from the open end, which faces the ocean, that we're able to see enough to write.

Where to begin? There's so much I want to share with you. I hope you'll get the chance to read this and consider it. When I was a teenager, life's "Big Issues" were not in my thoughts much. Later, in college, I began to look at things a bit more deeply. I never had occasion to talk about anything of significance with my grandfather, who died when I was in junior high. Oh, how I wish I had *my* grandfather's wisdom to think about then! Oops, I see that I'm rambling again! Can't erase and start over, so —

We thought it would be good for us, morale wise, to write letters with the expectation, or to be more truthful, the hope that someday they would be read. If we survive here on this rocky island long enough, you should have a lot to read. We're ever hopeful that you might someday read them.

Words cannot convey how much I miss those occasional talks with each of you. You seemed, as you matured, to be learning to be open and candid with others. That means a lot to me. I feel most people, and men seem to be the worst, cannot, or will not share their inner feelings nor listen compassionately to what others share with them. Perhaps some of what I write in the letters that follow will strike a chord within each of you and provide some encouragement, insight and guidance as you move into adulthood. Please, if you do nothing else with what I write, open your hearts and minds and try to get a sense of where I am coming from.

Although I can no longer influence your young lives, and maybe never will see you again, I can only pray that these letters will someday reach you. My love and prayers are with you always.

Enough of that.

Harry commented that one thing he missed terribly was people. Melanie responded, "Well, Harry, what about us? We're people!" He smirked and replied that yes, of course he knew Melanie and I are people, but there are only two of us in his new, limited world. He regrets that his "world" has shrunk to only two friends. All three of us feel the same. That got me to thinking. Based on what you kids and I have seen of each other, I imagine that you may already know what I am about to write, but let me write it anyhow.

<u>Always look for the good</u> in the people you come in contact with. Look for what is best and noblest and kindest in them. And guess what; that is what you will see; that is what you will encourage in them; that is what you will bring out of them. If you're thinking as you read this, you will of course ask, but, Grampa, what about bad people? There is evil in the world, and unspeakably evil people who commit horrific acts: murder, rape, torture, and cruel abuse. That's true. But look around you. They are the tiny minority. Perhaps bad things will happen to you, perhaps done by an evil person. I pray such will not happen to you, of course. But you have a shield, a cone of protection, if you will. And it is simply this: you are always in God's care and keeping. Look for goodness in those around you, and you will not be disappointed.

What I wish for you to get out of this letter, and those that will probably follow, is a sense of who I am and what I believe. Maybe then you can incorporate, as least some of, it into your lives, as I trust you will.

You are good kids, growing into productive and kindly adults. I am writing to you with the goal of assisting you in making choices that will enrich your lives and make them glow with inner happiness.

And now, a little about our existence here.

Because we have not the slightest idea when, or if, we will be rescued, we have decided to avoid consuming any of the canned and packaged edibles. We will survive as best we can on whatever we can find living on the island. If, on occasion we feel we must open something, we will do so, but reluctantly.

We are busy much of the day exploring, gathering canned goods that show up from time to time from our wreck, and examining plants. Whenever we find a new plant, or blossom, or fruit of any sort, we pick a few samples and take a very tiny taste. Then we wait to see what happens, if anything. We also nibble leaves and roots in the same manner. And we've tried some seaweed, too, pretty yucky stuff, but if we can get nourishment from it, flavor doesn't matter! Melanie is keeping a log, with drawings, of each plant and the date, time, and results of our little nutrition experiments. Some twenty years ago she took a "Survival Foods" seminar, at a college near the hospital where she worked, in which the instructor described how to test plants for edibility. She is using what she learned then to do the experiments here. Gradually we should learn what flora is edible, as our survival depends on it. We're just getting started, but we must discover what is edible and what is not. Sometime in the next week or so we will get more systematic about gathering sea plants and begin sampling them and adding them to our "experimental nutrition log." When we have a fire going, we will boil some of those plant materials to see if they taste better or if the negative effects of some of them are lessened by cooking.

We just ate our meager supper. We ate some raw seagull meat, several raw clams, and some of what we are calling sea lettuce... No fire, so we ate everything cold.

There are reasons for not having a fire. In the first place, it seems to be very rainy and wet here, and we do not have a covered place to build and maintain a fire. Consequently, any fire we build will be extinguished when hard rains fall. Secondly, we only have those three Butane lighters. When they run out, we will have no way to start a fire. We will struggle to stay alive on what the island provides. It is July, and we know winter will come. Judging by how chilly the weather had been, we must assume that winter will be very cold. Because we fear there is a chance that we will still be here when cold weather strikes, fire will have to wait.

The rain has let up a little now, so we will put our letters away, don our rain gear, and go exploring, while it is still light enough to see. We have agreed that exercise will be important to our health and our survival, so we try to go for a long walk every day; much of it involves clambering over rocks and stone ridges. As we walk we watch for anything that might contribute to our survival. Somewhere I read or heard this: "The body is the temple of the spirit." Take care of your body, being careful what you do to it, what you put into it, and how you care for it, remembering that it houses your soul, that which is Eternal within you.

Love, Grampa

Dear Grandkids:

Today was extraordinary! I can't wait to tell of it!

Not long after sunrise and a skimpy breakfast of raw seagull eggs, washed down with rainwater we had bottled yesterday, we hiked to the top of the island to see if we could see any boats. Sadly, the fog thickened so that we could see to land's end, but barely beyond the last rocks sticking up out of the water beyond the surf.

Let me explain about the seagull eggs. I hesitate to put this down on paper, but feel I must. We want to last for as long as necessary, so, at Melanie's instigation, we have taken to "trying out" various nourishment ideas. I remember enough from my Escape and Evasion Training early in my army career to know a little bit. As I wrote earlier, we take small tastes of items, leaves, berries, and seaweeds for example, and wait to see if they make us ill. And Melanie, being a nurse, has a pretty sound understanding of human nutrition.

Anyhow, here goes: We have learned to eat raw seabird eggs! At first we had huge difficulty when we opened eggs to find partially formed embryos inside. We gagged on them and vomited them right back up. But we persevered and now, like primitive savages, we are able to get them down. Melanie insists that the amount of protein in them is worth the (ugh!) effort.

Now here's the exciting part of our day. Over near the larger of our sandy beaches, I noticed a huge number of gulls swooping and calling. We watched them for a while, and then strode briskly in that direction to try to see what was going on. Couldn't believe what we discovered when we got to the edge of the shore: they were diving frantically into the surf and coming up with fish! Melanie, who has the sharpest eyes among us, exclaimed, "There are fish swimming up with the waves, then flopping their way back to deeper waters, thousands of them!" The gulls, by the hundreds, frantically screeching and diving, did their part to create a melee of sound and motion.

"The net!" Harry cried. While Melanie stayed and watched, mesmerized, Harry and I ran to our shelter and returned with the fish net. At Harry's suggestion I snatched up several raingear pants and jackets and brought them along. After a few moments with Melanie we had a plan.

We took turns running into the surf, casting the net and letting the fish wriggle down the sloping beach into it. Then we dumped the catch into a rain jacket. We knotted the sleeves to keep them in. The fish, thousands of them, it seemed, were behaving in as frenetic a manner as the gulls. For that matter, so were we, laughing and shouting as we netted fish after fish after fish. After the jackets were filled, we filled the raingear pants, with the legs knotted, of course. It was a wild, uncontrolled madhouse of gulls, fish, sweeping and receding waves, and us. The fish came in several sizes, all less than a foot long, some as short as three inches.

After a couple of exhausting hours, we dragged our catch back to the shelter, dumped them into a five foot wide hollow uphill from it, where we knew they could not escape. Note: the little brook that runs under the stone floor of our gully shelter flows out of the bog I mentioned earlier. Some thirty feet up from our shelter is a natural pool. We added rocks and mud to keep the fish in it. Then we hurried back to the beach. By mid afternoon, hunger, which we had forgotten all about in the excitement, got our attention and we did what any raw-seagull eating predators would do; we each bit into a live fish. They were quite tasty. It was kind of like eating little sardines, only they were less oily. Instant sushi!

We made two more trips back to "the pit" before exhaustion overcame us and we collapsed in three wilted heaps.

We were "stuffed to the gills" with all but the gills and heads of the little fishes.

I am writing this note with a hand cramped from its exertions. So will close for now.

What an exciting day this was!

Love, Grampa

Dear Grandchildren,

A short note to finish my fish story.

By the time today was coming to an end we must have had at least five hundred fish flopping around in the rock pool, which collects runoff and holds it for several days! Now we were puzzled: what to do with them? Obviously as long as they were alive, we could dine on raw fish to our hearts' content. But they would not live here forever.

After some discussion we decided to make a big fire some five feet across, and let it die down to a bed of coals. While we awaited that result, we gathered a massive amount of kelp and other seaweeds, hauled fish out of the pool, beheaded them, and wrapped them in the seaweed, in bundles of half a dozen of more each. Only slightly hampered by the gathering dusk, and overheated by the hot ashes, we scraped the old fire down to the bottom and threw in dozens and dozens of wrapped packets of fish. Then we covered the packets with the hot ashes, some of it still containing flaming bits of wood, and crawled into our shelter to fall into deep sleep.

I should note that wet footwear has been a problem, until we came up with our Brilliant Footwear Plan. Melanie, as usual, was concerned about our health and wellness, only this time about our feet. With feet that are almost constantly wet, even with the many socks we have in our possession, we are in danger of developing the dreaded trench foot or similar ailments. Consequently, we now use boots from our dead comrades whenever we are wading, gathering food from the sea or looking for items washed up from our wreck. Their boots are not good fits, but that's of little consequence when stumbling around in a few feet of water. At all other times, we go barefoot when it is warm enough to do so, or wear our own boots and socks, which are now fairly dry.

Tomorrow we will retrieve the cooked fish from the ashes of the fire. Our plan is to gorge ourselves with them until they rot and become inedible. Feast or famine, as they say!

Love, Grampa

Dear Grandchildren,

Harry came back from a long walk to the western end of the island, grinning from ear to ear and carrying a large sea bag! Hooray! Apparently one of them made it to land! Inside was Ferdinand Armstrong's wallet, so we know to whom it belonged. He was one of our fellow Adventure Travelers. Ferd's body was not among those that washed ashore here. He was a big man, but his clothes, even if they are too large for any of us, will help provide protection if we are here long enough to wear out what we have with us. We found a snorkel face mask among the items in his bag, plus a pair of fingernail clippers, his toothbrush, which we will have to share, and a bottle of Tylenol. We've been going nuts with our long fingernails and toenails! The find cheered us up momentarily, although we have been struggling with depression since we arrived, for obvious reasons! Who would ever think that fingernail clippers would be a cause for celebration?

As a result of all that has occurred, and after a lot of discussion, Melanie, Harry and I have arrived at the obvious conclusion that our survival will depend very heavily on our attitudes. If we give up and sink into despair, we will surely sicken and die. The will to live is not enough; we must work diligently to remain positive, optimistic, cheerful, and caring of each other. Our daily goal, upon awakening, is to smile and greet each other with a hug. Then we plan our day, and make ourselves "get going." It would be so easy to lie here together in our humble "shelter in the gully" and feel sorry for ourselves. After all, we have little hope of being rescued soon, especially as we have no idea where we might be, how remote this little island might be from any other human activity. It is often foggy. When it is somewhat clear, we scan the horizon, hoping to see a boat, but, so far, without success. We think we see a smudge way off on the horizon that might be another island, but it might as well be as far away as the moon for all the good it will do us!

And suddenly the light dawns! I know what I want to write about! So here goes…

You live in a crowded world, where, strangely enough, many people are lonely. At least that is what the three of us have decided, in our Godlike wisdom! Our "world" contains only three people! Years ago, at a nine week chaplain school, during a spontaneous late night group discussion in our barracks, we were given a bit of wisdom. We were happily going on and on about our mission in the world: "to bring God to men and men to God", to save souls, to persuade soldiers to be religious; you know, that sort of thing. After a while, I thought I might need hip-waders to make my way through all the well meaning B.S., mine included. In a moment of tired silence, the rabbi in our group spoke softly, saying, "If I can just be a little ray of sunshine to the people I meet each day, I feel I will have done God's work." I have carried those words with me for all these years, convinced that, despite all our clergy high mindedness, he was right.

First and foremost, <u>we must always and everywhere be a source of positive, cheerful optimism</u>. As Tom Dooley wrote many years ago, we should try to "light one little candle" in our sometimes dark and dreary world. Look him up some time.

Think about it, kids: How many of your friends at school light one little candle of friendship, kindheartedness, and optimism? From what you have told me, there is a lot of bullying, complaining, and pessimism among teenagers. I recall that in my high school, there were many who seldom smiled unless they were sharing jokes or unkind comments about kids that were on the outside of their little clique. And, their laughter was often merely on the surface, a part of the discomfort of being a teenager in world they didn't really "get" yet. Maybe you have seen the same sort of thing. I still remember what it felt like not to be in any of the cliques in my high school. As you know, you can be part of the inner group one day, and excluded from it a week later. Teenagers are so fickle!

And, of course the news each day, if you bother to read it or hear it, is more about violence, disaster, war, and famine than it is about love and kind deeds. Sometimes optimism seems kind of silly, doesn't it?

So? Here's my advice to you, dear ones: Work at developing a way of living and looking at life that will help to create a brighter world. When your days on this earth end, will you have brought a little light and happiness and joy into the lives of those you pass? Or will you have helped to diminish the hope and happiness of your part of the world? A heavy burden, I know, but one I pray you will willingly shoulder.

Our religion, and many others, insists: "Love your neighbor as yourself." What better way to love your neighbors than to be a bright spot in their lives? Even when things go sour, as they will do at times, try always to be an open, caring, happy, friendly person. Don't be afraid to be an optimist or to share that optimism with those around you.

Well, that's what I am trying to do here on this godforsaken island in the middle of nowhere. Harry and Melanie are also writing letters on the same topic.

So our restricted little world here is going to be a place where each day is greeted with thankfulness to be alive, and love is shared. As it says in the Bible somewhere, "Go thou, and do likewise."

And, guess what? Fish for dinner!

Love, Grampa

Dearest Loved Ones,

We had fish for our meals today, surprise, surprise.

I will tell you about our rather awkward day. Melanie suggested that we should go up to the depression at the top of our island and see if there are any earthworms. "Why?" Harry asked. Her disgusting reply was that we may well have to eat worms for sustenance if we are here long enough! Now that's a real yuck!

After some 25 days we have noticed a bad smell, and it is us! So Nurse Pickett presented an ultimatum: cleanliness!

There are many indentations in the larger rocks and rock ledges. Over the eons, wind and weather have apparently sculpted them. Some of the depressions are six to ten inches deep, or thereabouts, and several feet long. In the late morning, we stood looking at several of them that happened to be clustered in one small area. Harry and I agreed with Melanie that they sort of looked like miniature bathtubs. To which she commented, with a crooked grin, "from now on they *are* bathtubs!" With that, handing Harry a scrap of cloth from her pocket, she ordered him to strip, sit and scrub. His protests of modesty were to no avail, as she remarked that she was a nurse, after all. "Not to worry, Harry," she commented, "I've seen it all before." He fussed that the air was too cold, but I replied that the temperature seemed to be around sixty-five degrees, and, after all, we were finally enjoying a sunny day. He scowled at me, and after some blushing, stripped and sat himself down in the pool. I pooh poohed his complaint that the water was ice cold, until it was my turn! When I emerged from my "bath," Melanie quipped, "Hey, mister, your birthday suit needs ironing!" After a fit of the giggles, no doubt brought on by embarrassment, Melanie took her bath.

I shall pause here to make a comment. I'm sure you will be shocked at reading all this, assuming you ever get the chance. I'm hoping that some day you will all read our letters. The three of us have agreed we should try to assume that our letters will reach you, someday, somehow. We must avoid letting despair creep in, when we wonder if all this writing is a waste of time. Believe me when I tell you that there is no place for modesty when three wrinkled senior citizens find themselves shipwrecked on a barren island!

We each scrambled back into our odiferous clothes and sat in the sun. It seemed counter productive to get back into smelly clothes, so we decided, then and there, to have a "laundry day". We went back to our shelter, gathered up socks, underwear and clothes we had worn during our stay, then went to the pool where we had stored the small fish we caught and took turns sloshing the clothes around using a broken oar we had salvaged. Laying everything out in the sun, we huddled under separate blankets and spent several pleasant hours talking about keeping clean, hygiene in general, and what we were learning about "survival edibles."

Tomorrow we will gather up the clothes we salvaged from our dead fellow travelers and use the same method to clean them up for our future use. We have quite a collection of wearing apparel, which we had semi dried and stored inside our shelter. The shelter has grown as we scrounged bits and pieces of our boat, and created small cubbyholes to stash things out of the weather. It is very cramped, what with all the clothing, personal items and shrink-wrapped pads of paper jammed around the edges of our sleeping space. I should add that the clothes still smelled after washing, there being no soap, of course. But they were less repulsive than before being put through our primitive laundry.

We discussed our health again this evening. We must cover every inch of this island as we search for anything that may help us continue to exist. Harry says the exercise of walking about will be good for us, helping ours hearts and lungs to stay healthy. Melanie thought that moving rocks aside to make easier walking (and carrying) might be a good idea. The bending, reaching and lifting will provide beneficial physical activity. None of this will be easy, as we are always hungry, and can see that we each have already lost a few pounds.

There's a message here for you: take care of your body. Respect it. Do not abuse it. It's the only one you will get. Please, I implore you: <u>never</u> get caught up in drugs or excessive drinking!

Tomorrow, while our collection of clothes is drying (if the sun stays with us, that is) we will try to lay out a long, walking course that avoids much of the treacherous rocky areas, so we can move briskly for a half hour each day. I remember when I was on active duty, hearing former POWs tell me that they could walk even when nearly starving. Oh happy thought! We shall see!

Love, Grampa

Dear Grandkids,

More about our walking paths. It occurred to us that we should make many paths that take us through all the parts of the island. Having good footing on them will not only be safer, but it will make it easier to carry any forage materials we find.

Yesterday morning we discovered a new plant. We were walking along the northern shore, examining the "wheat" grass, when Harry called to us. "Come here! I think I've found a plant we have not seen before." We squatted with Harry and looked at the leafy green plant with white blossoms.

Melanie, of course, suggested that we must sample it and, hopefully, add it to our list of edible plants. I was invited to be the guinea pig for this one, so I chewed a leafy part. It wasn't exactly delicious, but it went down okay and I did not suffer any discomforts as the day progressed.

Exploring further, we found many clumps of the plant, some of them under water, with their fronds moving gently in the mild ocean swell near shore. We hope this will prove to be a workable food source!

We cut off a foot long bundle of the plant and headed back to our shelter. As we walked, Melanie kept handling the plant and pursing her lips. "I've seen pictures of this plant somewhere."

While we were eating supper, she remembered and reminded us of the "Survival Foods" course she took some twenty years ago at a college near the hospital where she worked.

Now, I must comment here, that Melanie often surprises Harry and me with her phenomenal memory. She dredges up medical terms, names of people from the past, addresses, of friends and even phone numbers. So it was not a great surprise when she suddenly had an "Aha!" moment about a plant.

"This," she exclaimed proudly, holding up one of the plants, "is commonly known as scurvy weed," and she proceeded to spout its Latin name: cochlearia officinalis. She helped me with the spelling just now. As you might imagine, Harry, amazed at her memory feat, almost choked on the strip of seagull meat he was chewing. I was fortunate to have an empty mouth at the time.

I have trouble remembering what day of the week it is. And I could not recall the names of many of our fellow travelers. But Melanie, of course, did. It was she who managed to piece together the names and some personal information about our fellow travelers, and then write it all down. Her notes will provide information to anyone who might find our campsite someday.

Back to the scurvy weed; you can imagine how exciting this was for us. If she was correct, and who could doubt that she was, we had an important nutritional contributor to our long term health. We hadn't even thought about scurvy…teeth coming loose, and all that. It appears as though we will not have to face that illness if we are here long enough for it to be a factor.

You just never know what awaits you around the next corner in life!

Love, Grampa

Dear Grandchildren,

I have reread my letter of July 20th, and I realize I left something vital out of it. I simply said that we decided to adopt a positive outlook on our lives here. Well, it was not that simple. We did not just have a casual conversation and make that decision. I feel that I must tell you some of the details of that matter.

That Saturday began with a meager breakfast, as usual. Not long after we ate, Harry, who seemed especially preoccupied, shook his head and said something like, "I'm going to take a walk." We watched him as he worked his way among the rocks, below the cliff to the east, above the high tide area. His posture seemed slumped, his movements slower than usual. So Melanie and I continued to observe him, and commented to each other that something was not right. Eventually when he was a tiny figure in the distance, he stopped and turned toward the ocean. He just stood there. Then he sat, lowered his head on to his hands and remained motionless. He was way too far away for us to see any details.

Melanie asked, "Do you think he's all right? You don't suppose he might do something foolish do you, like walk into the water and let himself go under?" I was thinking along the same lines.

"Maybe we'd better go to him," I ventured. So we stood and headed his way.

Before we got to him he looked up at the ocean, turned his head our way, stood, and began walking toward us. We met not far from where he had been sitting. His eyes were red, obviously from weeping, his cheeks wet with tears.

So we talked deliberately, gently, and quietly together. He said he had been thinking about just ending it all: wading out among the rocks and letting himself slip under the light surf. Melanie and I were right in our assessment of his mood, you see. Then and there, the three of us admitted, to our sense of hopelessness, our fear that we would never be found, that we would die on this godforsaken rock pile. We stood together, tears streaming down our cheeks.

And we hugged, like one of those "group hugs" that are so superficial and of little meaning. But our group hug was a hug of souls intertwined together, of accepting our mutual reliance on each other, of acknowledging that we were in a very difficult situation. Our bodies pressed together and our arms around each other, merely symbolized the depth and breadth of our compassion for each other, and our dependence on each other.

It was a little later, as we worked our way back to our forlorn little shelter that we had our talk. It was then and there that we agreed that, as Harry put it, "We must work continuously to remain positive, optimistic, cheerful, and caring of each other".

So, you see, we did not arrive at that conclusion lightly or easily. It was born out of despair and then affirmed with the certain knowledge that if we did <u>not</u> live that way, we would surely weaken, wither, and perish. It was a life-affirming, necessary, and practical decision.

Let's hope it works in the time that lies ahead of us.

Love, Grampa

Dear Family,

After our long morning walk, Harry suggested that we try to wade around where the wreck lies, see what we could find. The tide being low, the surf almost nonexistent, and the hazy day warm, somewhere near 70° we think, we dressed in our warmest, and driest, for the moment clothes, wriggled into our life vests, donned our ill-fitting wading shoes, and struggled into our rain gear.

The icy water at first took our breath away, made us shiver involuntarily. Then the water encapsulated under our rain gear, warmed slightly and we worked our way over and around rocks until we were chest deep. Harry used the snorkel face mask to bend and look into the water. Not sure what to do next, Melanie and I cupped our hands over the surface of the water and tried to peer into the depths. Melanie spoke a mild obscenity, immediately explaining that she was entangled in some kelp. But it wasn't kelp; it was white, synthetic rope. The three of us worked at tugging as much of the tangled mess toward shore as we could, which was not easy, as it was apparently twisted around rocks, and parts of our broken ship. Standing together amid tangled coils of rope, much of which was somehow anchored down in the water, we stopped and appraised the situation. Harry reached inside his rain gear and retrieved the large army knife with the serrated blade, unwrapped it and pulled himself under water. When he surfaced, a long minute or so later, he told us what he had accomplished. He had hauled himself down a length of rope. When he arrived at a jagged section of the hull, he found the line hopelessly tangled, cut it and returned to the surface. Encouraged by the partially freed bonanza, we worked together for an hour, and were able to free a mass of line that undulated gently around our legs. Note that sailors call it "line".

Once on shore, shivering uncontrollably as a result of being in the water so long, we untangled the mess and discovered that were now the proud owners of several lengths of rope. Now that it was on land, we could call it rope. We measured the pieces by extending segments from nose to finger tips, assuming that each segment was about three feet. We now possessed seven lengths of rope: the longest about thirty feet, and the shortest, maybe six and a half feet!

I'm sure we will find many uses for this newfound treasure!

By now it was well past noon, so we stripped out of our wet outfits, laid them about on warm rocks to dry, dressed in warm dry clothes and hiked to the steep cliff face to take part in an egg hunt. We have little knowledge of ornithology, so I cannot tell you whose eggs we found and stole. But I can tell you that the dozen eggs were quickly consumed, raw, naturally, along with some bitter little berries we harvested on the way back to our shelter.

Which brings me to today's little lesson for you. <u>Never take anything for granted</u>, for you never know when it will be gone. Enjoy your family, your home, your television, your cell phone and all the other things in your lives. Be aware of how lucky you are to have a car in which to get places. Revel in the luxury, yes, I said luxury, of cooked food, and the semi-certainty that you will be able to have more tomorrow, and the next day, and the next. And, of course, celebrate your siblings and parents, your cousins and uncles, your friends and neighbors. "Here today, gone tomorrow" has a special impact when you're shipwrecked on a rocky island with only two other people for company! The ancient Epicureans advised themselves to "eat, drink, and be merry, for tomorrow you may die." Good advice if you don't take it too superficially. Appreciate the important things in life, in addition to food, drink and friends, things like, love, honesty, good deeds, health, religious faith, and noble goals.

Permit me to interrupt myself here. I just thought of something Wow! A thought! "Treat it kindly, it's in a strange place," as my mother used to say. Over the course of many years I have had the benefit of many friends of many different religious persuasions: Roman Catholic Priests, Fundamentalist Christians, Rabbis, one Buddhist, two Hindus, a Japanese Shinto believer, and several Muslims. With all of them I have listened with an open mind and heart, desiring to learn as much as I could from them. It has been a rewarding journey of the spirit! A few of them, firm believers in their faith's sacred book, have told me that my faith was merely a brand of "watered down" Christianity. I dissented from their opinions, arguing that one can hardly be accused of having a "watered down faith" when he or she is firmly convinced of the existence of a spirit world, a God over all, life after death, and the need to love one's neighbor as oneself. And I would add this: we must practice these beliefs in our daily life. To which they, perhaps reluctantly, agreed! So keep this open mindedness idea in mind as you read my letters, please.

I write all this, as you will know if you ever get these letters, from the depths of a loving and aching heart. Oops, I am breaking the rule Melanie and Harry and I have agreed upon: no wallowing in self-pity. So I will give my moist eyes a swipe, end for now, and go sit outside with my friends to watch the day turn into night.

Love, Grampa

Dear Grandchildren,

We have finished a cold, skimpy supper of canned green beans and raw bivalves, some sort of clam-like sea creature, which we gather from the shallows at low tide.

Great news! Yesterday afternoon, while Melanie and Harry were walking in the rain on the other side of our island, they saw a large, rectangular object among the rocks. Turned out it was a severely damaged packet of four inch thick Styrofoam, containing six four by eight sheets! They were battered, some broken, and badly stained, probably because the bundle had been afloat for a long, long time. Most likely blew off some ship. Who knows?

It was as though God was watching over us! Here was a chance to insulate our little four by eight foot shelter in the gully. So today we went to work. We were able to cut and shape the Styrofoam, using the knife, our bare hands and the sharp edges of clam shell halves. Then we attached the shaped pieces from ceiling to floor inside our little shelter. We used seagull bones and small pieces of driftwood as pegs to fasten it together and keep the edges of one piece aligned with the edges of the next one. We also unbraided some of the rope and used it, sparingly. We are using as little as possible as we don't know what other needs things it may be used for. As a matter of fact, we try to be frugal with everything, hoarding things for a future we cannot predict. We did not finish the insulation job today, so we slept under two sheets of Styrofoam leaned together into a kind of pup tent, inside out shelter.

Today was cold, must have been around 40°. And this is still July!

Today's lesson in a nutshell, expect the unexpected. Who knows, it may be a good thing. Or it may be a bad thing. As the saying goes, "Hope for the best, expect the worst, and take what comes." The value is in being somewhat prepared for the unexpected so it will not blindside you. Life is an adventure! Don't we know it! Embrace it and run with it, wherever it takes you!

Now back to my story about our now cozier shelter. You may wonder where we got the seagull bones. Melanie netted several seagulls with that piece of fishnet she found. The gulls usually let us walk within a few feet of them, now that they seem to have accepted us in their midst. One can simply throw the net over a bird or two to capture them. Of course it usually takes more than one toss! Also, they often dive-bomb us when we walk among their nests. Melanie discovered that if she threw the net into the air as a dive-bombing gull swooped down; it sometimes would fly into the net and become entangled. From there it was easy to subdue and kill it. And yes, we killed them, partially cooked them on our Sterno stove, and ate them. We may try eating them raw, as we must save that fuel. We may need it come winter! I can imagine you saying, "Oh, gross!"

Harry suggested that we cannot go on cooking on our Sterno stove, as we will run out of fuel. We will use the Sterno to light driftwood fires from now on.

Do you remember the periwinkles we used to gather on the rocks at the seashore? Then we boiled them, used toothpicks to pull them from their shells, and dipped them in melted butter and ate them. We see millions of them on the rocks everywhere, and we are able to cook them in boiled seawater by using an already opened can as a pot. We place the can of seawater in the coals and wait for it to boil, and then put the periwinkles in it. But, alas, no butter to melt! I wish we had a larger pot.

Harry tells us that he was member of the local Polar Bear Club up in Michigan where he lived. Says if he went swimming through a hole in the ice, he ought to be able to dive to our wreck here. We discouraged that idea, reminding him that we had no warm dry place for him to retreat to when he comes out of the icy water. I'm sure this matter will come up again!

Tomorrow we will wander among the seals and see how close we can get. So far, they pretty much seem to ignore us as we walk among them.

As you will recall, we are hoarding our canned goods, with worried concern for what the long term future may hold. So for now there will be very few cans opened.

We don't know what will be available come winter here, if we're still here, and if we're alive.

Guess that's it for this letter. I fold each letter into a very small rectangle and stuff each one inside a slot in the Styrofoam ceiling to keep it dry.

The little slots with edges of folded paper provide "decoration" above me as I lie here. Hopefully tomorrow I can get back to sharing my thoughts about life in another letter.

Love, Grampa

Dear Grandchildren and my children,

Fog rolled in this afternoon and along with it a light drizzle. When we came home from our fitness hike, we did a little touch-up on our shelter, trying to improve its stability, then sat and tried to look ahead. When we see the sun again, we will try to dry everything out, for the umpteenth time. Things get wet, damp, and mildewed in the rain and fog. Maybe we can create a sheltered driftwood pile so it won't get so wet in the rains.

I have relearned a lesson during these past thirty-four days. Human beings are precious beyond measure! You soon come to realize that when you are one of three people left in the world. For that's what it is like for us here; we are, in effect, the last three people in the world. I pray that you will realize, early on in your lives, how vital positive human contact is, and focus your attention on treating everyone around you like gold! The world I left behind was one in which many people seemed to remain aloof or aggressive and hostile toward one another. I was sometimes guilty of that! Don't let that happen to you. Even if some people mistreat you, try to forgive them. Always remember that angry, negative people have bigger problems than you. If you can smile and offer a helping hand and a kind word, you will be appreciated and the world will be better for your being in it. Always, even when you don't feel like it, be ready to listen with compassion and offer advice with love.

Here's how it looks to me, or it did when I was back among my fellow human beings. For most of us, our daily lives are places of safe routine. There may be stress, or hardship, or illness, or many other complicating factors. There may occasionally be extreme anger and even violence as friends and neighbors lose control and lash out. Crime may strike in our midst. But our daily existence is, generally, an arena in which we can live loving lives.

My father stressed the need for me to be a "gentleman:" polite, considerate, and caring. "Gentleman," he taught, is made up of two words: "gentle" and "man." That's the better way to relate to others. As a Boy Scout, I was challenged to be "trustworthy, loyal, helpful, friendly, courteous, kind, obedient, cheerful, thrifty, brave, clean, and reverent." What a better world it would be if more people lived like that! And the heart and soul of the matter is gentleness.

Every day we make a thousand little choices. The world becomes a better place, and we become better people if we choose to be guided by this rule: Be a gentle person! We choose, moment by moment, whether to ignore or greet someone on the street; to frown or smile; to curse or bless. Arguments become discussions when we approach difference of opinion gently. Tempers cool, voices soften, and the mind is freed to look at both sides, because the threat of losing face, or being defeated, is reduced. We are responsible, and we can act in ways that either make the world a gentler or a harsher place. The choices are ours, all day, every day.

Make no mistake about it: what you do has an effect on others. You smile and say hello and you brighten a life; you frown and walk on by, and you darken a life. You treat someone with respect and they feel good; scorn them and they feel rejected. Gain money or power at the expense of others and they are demeaned. Compete fairly and lovingly, and your success is clean and pure. "Laugh and the world laughs with you, cry and you cry alone." Yes, there are many people who "could care less" how they are treated, and many who don't give a thought to how their behavior affects people around them. But not you, please, not you!

Some day you will have a "Midlife Crisis"! Midlife crises can arrive any time: in our teens, in young adulthood, in old age. I wonder when yours will happen. Most often it hits around the time our children are grown up, or nearly so, and many of our goals have been achieved. It is then that we may find ourselves pausing to reflect on where we have been, and what we have really accomplished. The anger and hostility we have vented on others, over the years, leaves a sour taste in our mouths. The heights of power or wealth to which we have climbed, lose their glamour. We discover that we have been changed by what we have sought and how we have acted. And sometimes the net result is depressing.

On the other hand, we discover that when we have focused our lives on loving, gentle thoughtfulness, we have been changed by that focus. We come to those crisis points in our lives when we find ourselves asking, "What have I done with my life that's worth anything?" Then comes the flash of insight: if we have loved, really loved, openly, sincerely, thoughtfully, and warmly, then a sense of assurance grips us. We discover a kind of wholeness that has nothing to do with money, prestige, power, reputation (good or bad), health, or religious creed. It has everything to do with our sense of worth, and that sense of worth rests upon what we have done about our fellow human beings. If we've tried to love and be gentle men, or gentle women, we experience a sense of fulfillment. On the other hand, upon looking back on our lives, we may keep seeing where we have shut people out, setting their needs aside, or caring not at all for those with whom we have competed. If that is so, then we discover another kind of insight. We find that we feel somehow diminished, cheated by our own ambitions, duped by our own inadequate goals in life.

Oops! I see that I have rambled on long enough. Not only that, but it is getting dark, and we, of course, have no light source. So I will end now with apologies for being so long winded Can one be long winded on paper? Take what I have written to heart, for is it well-meaning and sincerely offered. I miss you, and a lump forms in my throat every time I come to the end of a letter to you.

Love, Grampa

DAY 35
WEDNESDAY, AUGUST 2ND, 2006

Dear Grandchildren,

The three day rainy spell has ended! The sun has been shining from a partly cloudy, clear blue sky all day! We agreed that the temperature at sunrise must have been near 60°, and has risen perhaps into the low 70's. Or is that just wishful thinking?

We dragged every item of clothing, and our blankets out onto the rocks, weighed them down so they won't blow away, and are letting Mother Nature dry things out for us, again. We have rigged two clotheslines up near the ceiling across the inside of our shelter. There is always some laundry hanging from them, socks in particular as dry feet are a major concern. The hanging clothes and dry socks are more important that empty space.

While the things were drying, we traveled the shoreline gathering all the driftwood we could find, and moving it well above the high tide line. There must be tons of driftwood: trees, branches, broken bits of lumber, some teak decking, and some pieces of wood from the coach roof and sides of our boat. We've even found some warped and damaged pieces of plywood. Who knows what ship those pieces might have come from? It will take us weeks to move all this potential fuel and building material up to dry ground.

We also dragged or carried a lot of it to our little campsite, and began to make a big stack. We're trying to arrange it in such a way that it is not a hopeless tangle when we need it. We don't know how long we will be stranded here or how cold winter will get, so we plan to assemble a huge pile of wood for fires when it is cold. We are also slowly building a three sided, U-shaped firepit, right in front of our shelter, partially in the gully and partially not, by rolling, dragging and carrying stones here, and then stacking them into a wall. It will take a while, but eventually we hope to have a four foot tall windbreak. Did I mention that we are on the windward side of the island?

Of course we expect more rain, as this seems to be a wet and foggy part of the world. We have had rain and/or fog for half the time we have been here. Sometimes the fog is a pea soup that prevents us from seeing more than a few feet; at other times it is more of a heavy haze that gives us fair visibility of most of our island. But when we look out to sea, the sky and the water blend together in such a way that there is no horizon and we have no idea how far we can see before it all becomes a gray impenetrable haze. We are hoping to contrive some sort of cover for the firepit so we can keep the flames alive when it is cold, windy, and rainy. Don't know whether to expect snow or not, but it seems likely.

This morning I got to thinking about how we tend to take other people's kindnesses for granted: things like gifts, meals, rides, invitations. I remember when, on a couple of occasions, one of you forgot to send a thank you note for a gift, one at Christmas, one a birthday present. Of course, I don't do something kind or thoughtful so that I will receive a thank you. But I

32

also must admit that it was a bit of a disappointment, a minor hurt, not to get one. So here's what I want you to consider: "Please" and "thank you" are fundamentally important words in our human experience. Fail to offer those words too often to someone, and they will give up on you. Maybe they'll stop giving kindnesses. Or maybe they'll continue giving, but with a little corner of sadness in their hearts because of your inconsiderateness. So? Remember, always, to say and/or write a thank you! It is never a mistake to do so!

You could make a little word pyramid with "I love you" on the bottom, "thank you" next, and "please" at the top.

The conscious attempt to remain positive and optimistic seems to be working. Harry and Melanie repeatedly comment about how the effort of doing this together has reduced the weeping spells we all have from time to time. As much as possible we avoid mentioning our feelings of despair, and focus on making a pleasant life here, and working at a hopeful attitude concerning a possible rescue. We may be here for a long, long time, so we are creating a mini civilization based on making the best of a difficult situation and seeding our experience with humor, bright outlook and a jaunty sense of adventure. We are "Adventure Tourists" after all! How many people get the opportunity to build a community like this? For that matter who would ever <u>want</u> to?

After a month here we have yet to see any kind of boat or ship. The frequent fog and poor visibility may be a factor, or maybe we are far from any routes taken by fishing boats or ships. Most days we can only see a limited distance. The haze and fog blends with the ocean waters to make it nearly impossible to judge how far we can see.

Love, Grampa

Dear Grandkids,

This morning in the early hours of darkness, we began talking about religious people and how they develop their personal faith. That led me to review my thoughts on the matter. So here goes.

How do we become religious? What prompts us to bother? The second question is an easy one: we know our bodies will die eventually, so we are concerned about what happens next. Is there a life after death, you know, that sort of thing. Some people worry about this, others are simply curious, some give it no thought at all.

Well, today I'd like to offer my thoughts on the first question. I'm sure you're aware of the many major religions and the thousands of religious sects. How do we become religious? With all the thousands of organized religions, and an infinite number of beliefs, practices, sacred writings and points of view, how do we arrive at ours? The answer is very simple and outlandishly divisive: We pick and choose what we will believe and what we will doubt. We do this choosing, with the noblest and highest of intentions, as we try to discover God's will for our lives. We choose, or have chosen for us, what great religious grouping we shall join, such as Christianity, Islam, or Judaism. We select major subdivisions as our own, such as Roman Catholic, or Protestant. Then we narrow our choice down to a denomination, for example, Episcopal, Methodist, and Church of God. Then our options become more specific: St. John's, Calvary Baptist, Main Street Community. In the process we narrow down what Sacred Writings we will follow, and how devoutly we will adhere to its teachings, the Bible, for example. We study our chosen Sacred Writing, seeking wisdom for the living of our earthly lives.

Let me share an example of what I'm writing about: I have friends [married couples] who are Christians who believe that The Bible is the <u>exact, literal, "written by the finger of God", word for word Truth.</u> Yet when they come to the Apostle Paul's guidance on the place of women, they choose not to obey. Told women should cover their heads at worship; they choose not to. Wives are instructed: "let wives also be subject in everything to their husbands", yet these married couples choose to be equal with their spouses in all things. I give this example not to disparage or ridicule their faith, for I am impressed by their devotion and loyalty to their "Sacred Book". They worship faithfully, and strive diligently to follow their Lord and the teachings of their Sacred Writing in every possible way. But they do make a few exceptions. In other words, they choose what they will believe and follow, even from within their most sacred Book! However small the divergent choices are, they demonstrate the fact that we all choose what we will believe; we select what dictates we will follow. It is our acts of choosing that lead to the growth or decline of our religious faith. We pick and choose our loyalties, beliefs, doubts, and sources of religious authority.

My point? Don't be sucked into the notion that someone's sacred book, The "Word of God" as they often describe it, has any more authority than another person's sacred book. There is no need to argue about whose written word is true and whose is not; indeed, there's no point to such discussions. Better that we open our hearts and minds to others and search together for meaning and purpose. Interestingly, most of the major religions I have studied stress the need to love our fellow human beings and to love God, Yahweh, Allah, or whatever name their God may be called.

Organized religion is good when it draws people together to seek spirituality, to provide mutual support, to organize acts of kindness, and to try to discern God's will for us. It is bad when it decides and declares that it has found the one and only Right Answer(s), for then it becomes a divisive force in a world that desperately needs unity.

Love, Grampa

Dear Grandchildren,

Today the surf was down to almost nothing, little wavelets lapping our rocky coast. We have been waiting for such a day, and it is finally here.

I have mentioned that Harry told us he was a member of a Polar Bear Club in Michigan. He told us he would make his dive on the wreckage today. Melanie's response was simple and to the point, "Harry, you're nuts!" I tended to agree with her, as the waters here are frigid, icy, brutal, foot numbing cold. But Harry was insistent. And, in his favor is the fact that the sun is out, although in a hazy sky. And it is fairly warm; I would guess somewhere in the high sixties, with only the gentlest of intermittent breezes. So I guess if someone is planning on a swim, today might be the day.

So we gathered things together in preparation for what Melanie and I considered an unwise activity. We used some of the rope to create a large drawstring bag out of the piece of fishnet; gathered blankets and laid them out in the sun. They would be for Harry when he came ashore. We built a driftwood fire in our three sided windbreak and placed a stack of wood within easy reach. By this time it was around noon, the warmest part of the day. It was time to get the show on the road.

After we stood around with our hands on our hips for a while, checking to see if we had thought of everything, we walked to the water's edge. Harry, stripped to his heavy sweater, sweat pants, and rain suit, glanced at the two of us bundled in all our gear: life vests under our slickers. Then we waded among the rocks until we were almost chest deep, which put Melanie in water almost to her shoulders. Harry stood briefly between us, while I tied a safety line around his waist, tying the other end to my left wrist. He smiled, pulled the snorkel mask down over his eyes and nose, faced out to sea, lowered his head and shoulders and headed for the bottom. The last we saw of him was a pair of legs and bare feet rising up out of the water and sinking out of sight.

Time stood still, until, after what seemed like forever, Harry bobbed to the surface ten feet to our right. "Move over this way," he commanded, and disappeared again. When he next rose to the surface, he swam the few strokes to us and handed Melanie a hatchet! He would later tell us he found it still attached to a piece of the cabin wall next to the first aid kit and fire extinguisher. Rather than bore you with a detailed account of each dive, I will simply list what he retrieved for us to put in the net bag: a ten pound bag of rock salt shrink-wrapped in several layers of heavy-duty plastic. Adventure Tours also does winter sailings, and the rock salt is for use on the decks and docks, or so we assume. We also now have stainless steel implements: dinner plates, mugs, knives, forks and spoons. It took him several dives to stuff the silverware in his pockets, come to the surface, and hand them to us. He also retrieved a Butane cigarette lighter, a cast-iron skillet, a cooking pot, and a sail bag with a huge brightly-colored spinnaker! He would have looked for more but by this time he was in rather bad shape. His legs were cramping, his lips were deep blue, and he was shaking uncontrollably.

We helped him to shore; he would never have made it without our assistance, as he could not stand, and was mumbling incoherently. His eyes were red and his skin was as cold as any ice I had ever touched. With one arm over each of our shoulders, and his feet dragging uselessly over the rocks, Melanie and I struggled to get him to the fire. After wrapping him in blankets and throwing more wood on the fire, we waded back to the fishnet bag and dragged it and the sail bag ashore.

Harry, lying in his cocoon of blankets, teeth chattering, eyes closed, his body shaking like a leaf in a storm, was semi-conscious at best. Melanie and I removed our wet clothes, quickly slid into dry shirts and pants, then crawled under the blankets, one on each side of him, and held him as close to our warm bodies as we could. We stayed that way for an hour, watching Harry as he seemed to slip into a coma. We were afraid we would lose him at that point. But, slowly, oh so slowly, he began to come around, at first staring at the hazy sky, then turning his head to each side to look at each of us. Melanie extricated herself from the blanket wrap, rummaged around in the fishnet and retrieved the cooking pot, which she filled with water and placed among the hot coals at the edge of the fire. When the water was hot enough she added some leaves, which we had discovered made a bearable, but bitter tea, and soon we had a pot of tea. Holding one of the stainless steel mugs to Harry's lips, and propping him up against the rock wall of the windbreak, we were able to get hot liquid into him.

Not waiting for our permission, Melanie opened some of our canned goods: Boston baked beans, Harvard beets, and chicken noodle soup. Remember, we had agreed to save our canned goods for winter, hoping we would not still be here by then! She proceeded to heat them by making a slit on the top of each can, then resting them in the coals, and, after a bit, served our first dinner on our stainless steel plates! It seemed strange and wonderful to use spoons and forks!

Harry could move on his own, so with our help, he dressed in every item of clothes he could fit on his chilled body, which included Ferd Armstrong's oversized sweater. Then he wrapped himself in rain gear, and pulled blankets over and around himself as he sat looking into the flames.

So, I sit here and finish writing this account of our very harrowing day. Melanie whispered to me at one point, "I really thought we were going to lose him." I had the same awful thoughts. But, unless Harry develops problems during the night, I guess there will still be three of us tomorrow morning. I pray so!

We are bushed, so I imagine we will crawl into our shelter soon and go to sleep; there will be no evening walk tonight!

I will close for now, adding my love for all of you and my longing to be with you. Maybe someday? One can only hope.

Love, Grampa

37

Dear Grandkids,

Well, we have been here for something like forty days and forty nights. Harry and I now sport beards, mine gray, his white. He reminds me of a stocky Santa Claus. Although we are always hungry, and have lost some body fat, we feel pretty good. Our long walks, pathway clearing, plant gathering, and wood hauling all seem to be working, along with our Melanie guided nutrition experiments. At the risk of repeating myself, I again strongly urge you to exercise and be fit.

Today we went for another walk among the seals. They seem to be getting used to our presence. They ogle us with their big round eyes, and manage to shuffle away slightly. But for the most part they seem to have accepted us as part of their community. If we stand still for a few minutes, they will ignore us, except for some of the young ones, who sometimes will flop over to us and sniff us. What a thrilling departure this is from viewing wild animals across fences, and moats, or through glass or bars!

We know that someday we may need to kill and eat seals. And we may have to try to learn how to cure their hides for warmth and shelter. It may be early August at the moment, but we can be sure that winter will come someday, and with it, cold and more hunger. Will the seabirds, which we call seagulls, for lack of any better knowledge, leave us as winter comes? If they do, one source of protein, their stringy meat, will be gone. So we plot and plan, and hope we will not have to harm any of these gentle mammals. It's much more enjoyable to walk among them filled with wonder and warm cuddly feelings.

We fail to understand how men can take part in "seal hunts" in which baby seals are clubbed, by the hundreds, for commercial gain. But, for our survival? Well, that may shed a different light on our docile friends in their water-repellant seal skin clothes. Sad thoughts.

Harry has never been hunting, nor has Melanie. Killing for sport or some sort of warped "prestige" is not in my value system. The three of us, it turns out, are gentle folks, squeamish about killing, and reluctant to even harbor thoughts of it.

Today, after our "seal walk," we continued on, and climbed the steep, rocky cliffs, where smaller cliff dwelling birds live. The startled birds rose with squawks and wildly flapping wings. There is no way we can net them, but we found a few eggs, and cute little hatchlings. We admired them and left them. For now we will subsist on the easy to catch seagulls, which often dive-bomb us when we walk among their nests. Of course, as I recounted in an earlier letter, that makes it easy to throw a net above our heads and snare them as they swoop by. Harry commented once that he had never eaten a dive-bomber before!

The top fifteen feet or so of the cliffs are nearly vertical and we have decided that the exhilaration of climbing them is not worth the risk of injury if we fall. Not too many emergency rooms nearby! We found some more of the little edible berries, so we picked hands full and stuffed them in our pockets to enjoy with our evening meal.

Love, Grampa

Dear Grandkids,

An incredible wind in the early morning hours! We can only guess at its velocity. Maybe eighty or ninety miles per hour? In addition to seriously frightening us, it did some minor damage to our gully shelter, which we thought was virtually impregnable!

When it had abated somewhat, to maybe forty miles per hour, we dragged some logs and laid them against the upper and lower ends of the gully, leaning them against the shelter and using some more of our precious rope to tie them down, then rolling rocks against the bases of them.

Surely that will take care of the wind damage threat!

I find that all this adversity aids in the development of the courage to do what needs to be done, when you simply feel like huddling down and weeping with fear. There's a mini-lesson for you: you can overcome fear by doing what needs to be done in spite of it. When you are afraid, make yourself think, then take some sort of action. The wiser the action you choose, the better, even though your hands shake with fright and you feel almost paralyzed by your terror. And always keep in mind that feeling completely defenseless <u>must</u> not freeze your mind; there is usually something you can do to improve your situation.

Face your fear head-on. Use your mind to look for something useful to do.

It's getting too dark to write, so I will end this note.

I love <u>all</u> of you!

Love, Grampa

Dear Grandchildren,

It may be that by the time you read these letters, you will be adults. Gulp! I will now turn my attention away from that thought and all that it implies about our rescue!

After three days of thick fog and wet condensation everywhere, the skies cleared and we had one of those incredible crystal clear days! That morning we took our long fitness and forage walk, and then had a small lunch. After lunch we climbed part way up the steep slope below the cliff and sat looking out to sea, enjoying the view.

Suddenly, Melanie, who has the best eyesight among the three of us, pointed out to sea and asked, "What's that?" We strained our eyes to see what had caught her attention. After a minute or so we could see a speck far off, near the horizon. She exclaimed, "I think it's a boat!" We stood, shaded our eyes with our hands, and leaned forward, as if getting a few inches closer, and a foot or two higher, we could see better. As we watched, the object seemed to have grown in size and moved slightly from right to left. With much excitement in our voices and pounding hearts in our chests, we decided that it was a boat. We shouted and waved our arms for a few seconds, then stopped, looked at each other in embarrassment, and continued to watch it, far, far off — so far that we could make out no details. Of course, we could not begin to see if any people were on deck. So they could not see us, either.

Harry suddenly exclaimed, "Fire! We need a fire, a signal fire!" We scrambled frantically down to our little campsite which sits some twenty five yards up the shore, above any likely high water. There we started gathering dried grass, which we keep in a bundle inside our shelter, small pieces of wood, a can of Sterno, and the Butane lighter. We rapidly assembled a small pile of flammables. We lit the Sterno, slid it into an opening in the dried grass, and it worked. As soon as the grasses caught, Harry used a stick to drag the Sterno can out and cover it. We are being very conservative about our supply, so we burn as little of it as possible. Within moments the twigs caught and we could add slightly larger pieces of driftwood. Within ten minutes, we had a blazing fire going. I ran to the water's edge and gathered a clump of seaweed that was lying above the tide. Racing back to the blazing fire, I added some of it, and heavy smoke rose into the air!

"Let's hope they see it!" Harry shouted. We looked back at the speck, a speck we had been staring at intently from time to time, a speck that grew slightly larger for a while. We waited. Adding more wood and seaweed to the blaze, we soon had a brilliant, smoky bonfire going. We tended the fire, watched the boat, and willed it's occupants to look our way, hoping they would see our smoky fire. An hour passed. The boat became a barely visible speck and then disappeared. You cannot imagine the despair that gripped us. We simply sat together in silence on a flat rock near the fire as it gradually burned itself down.

It was Harry who finally broke the silence. "We should have had a fire already laid and ready to light in case we saw a boat." We agreed, Harry muttering that hindsight was better than no sight.

It being late in the day, we went hunting for our supper, baked a dozen eggs and three freshly caught and dressed seagulls in the coals that remained from our fire, ate heartily, and then turned to our letter writing. We intentionally over cooked the seagulls, creating a dry, brown kind of "gull jerky", which we hope will remain edible for several days or maybe a week. This is all part of our experimentation with food preservation. We would like to improve on our current hand-to-mouth food existence! Tomorrow we will build a signal fire and have it ready to light. Our spirits gradually revived, and by the time we were enjoying our food we were back to our usual cheerfulness.

There is a message in this for you: Never give up hope. No matter how bleak things look, fight to regain a positive attitude and begin to seek a workable outcome. When you can't change things, sulking and feeling sorry for yourself only makes matters worse. Stupid as it may sound to you, it is better to hold hopes high then to give up. Someone once said, "It is always darkest before the dawn." So when you get discouraged or disheartened about things, go to work on your attitude and make yourself see the brightest possible side of the matter. Your lives will be better if you can do this; I guarantee it! Today we learned this lesson, most dramatically!

The other message, taught to every Boy Scout, is "be prepared." We didn't do very well at that, did we!?

It's getting too dark to see what I am writing, so I will close for now. I love you very much, even more so after our upsetting experience today.

Love, Grampa

My dear family,

Today we woke up to a chilly, thick, pea soup fog; not an uncommon experience. The good news was that it was not raining!

Instead of our usual brisk, morning walk, we crossed the island and made many trips dragging and carrying firewood to our campsite. Actually we do this a lot, and have amassed a huge pile of wood, in preparation for winter, which we fondly hope we will not be spending here! After lunch we lugged wood, twigs, and dry grasses from inside our shelter, up to the flat rock from which we had seen the boat yesterday. We put together a teepee of wood and twigs. We wrapped the dry grasses in a slicker we had taken from one of our dead travel mates, and crammed the bundle inside the fire cone. When, or if, we see another boat, we need only unwrap the grasses, add the Sterno can, and light the whole thing. While it catches we will bring some damp seaweed up from the shore. Note: there is always plenty of seaweed in clumps among the rocks near the high tide line. We "wasted" another slicker, using it to cover the teepee, and weighing the edges down with rocks. If we someday need the signal fire, we can quickly remove the slicker and let the more or less dry wood burst into flame.

Now all we need is a boat on the horizon, or closer, dear God!

After lunch consisting of raw sea lettuce, that's what we call it, and six of the baked eggs from yesterday, we lounged around and talked. The subject turned to people we had known, some good and some bad, and then into another general discussion about the nature of people. Are humans basically good? Or are they basically bad? That was after I brought up the common Christian doctrine of Original Sin.

Think about it: if you assume people are selfish, bigoted, mean-spirited, and sinful from birth, thanks to their Original Sin, where does that lead you? A teacher friend of mine told me about "The Rosenthal Effect," which, in essence predicts that if you expect kids to be slow learners, they often will be, and if you expect them to be bright and interested in learning, they often will be that, too! I ask you to apply that notion to the people around you.

On the other hand, if you assume people are basically good, and are trying to do the best they can with the situations and the lives they have been given, well, maybe that attitude on your part will help them to succeed, guide them to realize their better potential. Sure, you will be surprised, hurt, and disappointed from time to time when people do stupid or mean things. But you can handle that. And I ask you, can you handle the gloomy results of always assuming the worst in people? I see little benefit in assuming that the behavior of others is nothing more than a calculated ruse to obtain personal gains and "to Hell with the rest of you."

Let me go on record with you here and now: I do not believe in the truth of that Garden of Eden tale about a God who created man and woman to be ignorant of good and evil. Many

Christians, of course, believe Eden to be a true story. I find it hard to believe that Eve duped Adam into eating the forbidden fruit, and then God booted them out of the Garden of Eden. It seems to me that living there, in that "Paradise on Earth," would have been absolutely boring and pointless. This would be especially true as Adam and Eve aged, spending weeks and years with nothing to do.

No, dear grandchildren, I see our Creation as something entirely different: a simple statement that we are in some way made "in the image of God." Perhaps the story of the Garden of Eden is more about Adam and Eve placing blame for their actions elsewhere. Even today, "the Devil made me do it" is a common blame shifting technique!

So? What's in this for you? <u>Believe in the goodness of mankind!</u> Most of us are trying to do the best we can with our lives. It is most assuredly helpful if those around us encourage us and stand by us. A high school friend once said of our friendship: "I accept you as you are, while dreaming of what you may yet be." Even when I did stupid or counter productive things, he remained my friend. He was there for me when I realized I was moving in the wrong direction and made the effort to change and improve. Oh, yes, your grampa sometimes has done things that he ought not to have done!

Sure, there are evil people in the world. And why wouldn't there be; we have been granted enough freedom of will to choose bad and hurtful actions as well as good and kind ones! Certainly there are many influences that push or pull people into becoming "bad" people.

Oh, I almost forgot: We finally decided what to do with that spinnaker we found. It is huge; it must be eighty feet or more per side! We really could use it to cover our shelter at this point. But then we had a better idea: we need a way to signal any boats that might come by. We can't watch all points of the compass all the time, or even most of the time. If a fishing boat came anywhere near our island it might spot the bright colors of the spinnaker, if we could figure a way to make it visible from all sides. So we agreed that it would make a good signal!

After some thought, we came up with a plan. We lugged it, in its sail bag, up the back side of the cliff. Climbing there is a safer approach than trying to scale it from the front. It took a couple of hours to drape it over the rocky outcrop at the top. After that we labored to weigh it down with the biggest rocks we could carry. We don't want it blowing away in the next storm! So we have a bright signal that should be visible from every point of the compass. Seems huge standing near it; but we wonder how much it shows up from a mile or more out to sea.

With that, I will end this letter. It is almost time for the three of us to enjoy our evening banquet. Harry is cooking tonight and he claims to have a tastier than usual treat for us. On that matter I will "hope for the best, expect the worst, and take what comes!"

Love, Grampa

My dear Grandkids,

After giving some thought to possible topics for this letter, I came up with this: So called "religious people." Are they all alike? I've heard agnostics and atheists say things like this, "Religious people are all alike; I want no part of them!" I know that people rebel against churches for many reasons: dislike of the liturgy (forms of worship), disagreement with the beliefs required for membership, disillusionment at clergy behavior, disputes with members, and a myriad of other reasons. And I've watched, as you teens are dragged kicking and screaming to church, or as you are sometimes allowed to stay home. One of you even once said to me, "Church is for old folks, not for me!" Well, please bear with me as I tell you what I think. Don't forget, I am writing this for you kids, so, no matter how old you are, when, or if you read these letters, please read them with an open mind and love for your Grampa Gregg.

After reading what I wrote yesterday, I think I need to add something. People: are they good or are they bad? This "Original Sin" business bugs me, as you can tell. Obviously, since I keep coming back to it!

Back in seminary I was introduced to the notion of Man's Original Sin. Adam and Eve got kicked out of the Garden of Eden for eating the Forbidden Fruit. What nonsense! But then, one must remember that it is a myth, not an historical document. First of all, having been retired for years, I can tell you that wandering around in a paradise like garden with nothing to do would be boring and pointless in the extreme. Second, what kind of God would want to withhold wisdom from his creation? What would be the point of mankind living with no appreciation of good and evil, nothing to do, and no purpose in life? Third, what is the point of approaching our daily lives with a hopeless sense of our worthlessness, which the so called "Doctrine of Original Sin" seems to encourage?

What kind of world do we think we live in today? How are our opinions about it formed? Many streams feed this river of opinion. Certainly one stream is family and home environment. If we're brought up in a home atmosphere of negative attitudes, immorality, friction, or poor communication, or if the neighborhoods in which we grow up are filled with poverty, crime and violence, then our view of the world will be different from someone who grew up in a loving, positive family and neighborhood. The attitudes and actions of our peers also color our conception of what humanity is like.

As we mature and talk with others, we also share another common experience that has a strong influence on our world impression: news media. We are surrounded by it. Well, you are; I'm not! Television, radio, the internet, newspapers, and news magazines; it's all there for you. Most of us spend a considerable amount of time reading and watching the media. It doesn't take long before we realize that certain kinds of news sell better than others. We are wrapped in a newsworthy environment of murder, corruption, brutality, natural disasters. Our conversations often turn to these kinds of events, and our attitudes are shaped by them.

The difference between newsworthy and not newsworthy is quite obvious, when you think about it. Some years ago, two German tourists were shot on a freeway in Florida, and the world read about it and saw it on TV. A single parent neighbor five doors down the street has major cancer surgery. Her neighbor arrives before breakfast and gets the kids off to school, visits for a while, and returns that afternoon with dinner for the kids. But we never hear a word about that! We hear about the bad, but seldom about the good. Multiply this a thousand times over the course of a year and it is easy to understand why we develop negative attitudes about the world in which we live.

We are exposed to video clips of cops brutally beating a helpless victim; but we don't hear about the cop in the same town firmly and politely enforcing the law. We read of yet another woman killed by a husband who violates both a restraining order and human decency; but no media shares the gentle companionship of a hundred couples in the same town. We watch as mass graves, the final resting place of victims of unspeakable cruelty, are uncovered in distant countries; but we have little knowledge of the quiet heroism of people rescuing fellow human beings from danger. We view the anguished face of a parent whose son was gunned down on a city street; but we don't see or feel the rush of friends and neighbors who reach out, nor do we hear about the young men and women who, daily, avoid violence and seek friendship and fair play. We mumble in disgust as another politician or business leader is investigated for corruption and ethics violations; but we don't witness the politicians and business leaders who, with sincere dedication to honor and integrity try to build a better world for us. And on it goes. In our disillusionment, we wonder if morality and ethics are driven more by fear of getting caught than by personal integrity. We shake our heads in disappointment when leaders seem more concerned with being criticized and investigated, than in addressing their own personal failure to live by a higher standard.

Troubles abound, and our exposure to the news media only reinforces the idea that bad people are dominant and that good people are in the minority. If bad news is the tip of the newsworthy iceberg of human experience, does that mean it is also an accurate view of the larger and less visible cross section of humanity and life? We need to remind ourselves that what is not shown on the nightly news is what's at the other end of the scale. We don't see much of human decency and goodness in the news.

Reviewing what happens in our own individual lives, most of us find something quite different from what we see and hear in the media. When we experience personal tragedy and loss, we find ourselves surrounded by love: food is brought in, neighbors call, wonderful cards of sympathetic love arrive, and prayers are offered. We experience good things: a new home, a graduation, a baby is born, a promotion takes place. Amid those happy times, we are further lifted by congratulations and expressions of shared pleasure on our behalf.

Organizations and individuals reach out to the confused, the downtrodden, the homeless, and the discouraged. They do so through volunteering at soup kitchens, taking part in Meals on Wheels, providing help with all manner of confusing paperwork, from taxes to insurance forms, joining in church activities, participating in civic organizations, and simply doing a million daily acts of kindness. When we enjoy the company of friends, relatives, and neighbors, warm feelings descend upon us that have little to do with what we have read in the paper, or seen on TV. In all these things we are taking part in the huge, submerged part of the iceberg of human experience that seldom makes the news, but usually puts a spring to our step and a song in our hearts.

I have often thought of the simple, but fundamental wisdom of a little verse that a chaplain friend of mine, Dave Huffnor, once told me about: There was a poster behind the counter in Dorothy's Doughnut Shop in his home town, which read, "As you travel on through life brother, always make this your goal; Keep your eye upon the doughnut, and not upon the hole!" There is nothing wrong with positive thinking. It not only makes the world seem like a better place, it probably does make it a better place, for there really is a POWER to positive thinking.

There is a world of goodness and growth, compassion and kindness, trust and integrity waiting for you to see, to embrace, and to nurture. It is essential to your spiritual growth and development that you nurture a positive attitude toward life and an optimistic approach to spirituality. For most of us, it doesn't just "happen;" we must work at it. A serious athlete trains to develop the stamina and skills needed for success. A spiritual person must also work to do the same. It requires the expenditure of time, talent, and energy to achieve most worthwhile things in life. Developing a positive and effective spiritual orientation requires more than just "wishing it were so."

If I can give you nothing else, let it be a positive outlook on life and its possibilities. With that attitude you can make your small part of the world a better place for your having been in it!

Love, Grampa

Dear Family,

We have been here now for something like 49 days.

And today is, as my cousin used to say, "A Doozy!" We awoke in the early morning darkness to howling winds and driving rain. We bundled up and went for a walk before breakfast. Well, not really a walk, more of a stagger! Buffeted by winds and nearly deafened by the roar of huge surf, we stumbled around for an hour and then came back to our shelter. Extremely tired, we crawled inside, pulled the door shut, and settled in for the day. What door, you may ask. Last week Harry fashioned a door out of a driftwood reinforced piece of Styrofoam, made rope hinges, and created a simple slide bolt to hold the door closed. So we are cooped up in our very dark gully shelter, hearing the increasing gurgle of water running under our stone floor, and hoping that our carefully constructed home will not come apart in the wind, which we estimate is gusting near a hundred miles per hour!

We again braved the storm, in the middle of the afternoon, after the winds calmed somewhat. Harry suggested that we might find some things washed ashore by the high and wild surf. Melanie said we ought to wait until tomorrow, when things might have calmed down a bit.

"I'm surprised that one of the survival cylinders hasn't surfaced," said Harry. "You'd think they might have broken loose and floated to the surface." He was referring to the two canisters on deck, one to starboard, one to port. Each one contained a ten person inflatable life raft. Also each cylinder included energy bars, trail mix, vitamin tablets, water, signal flares, thermal blankets, flashlights, a compass, and other things that would contribute to survival. During our first weeks here, we watched eagerly for one to pop up to the surface. They are fastened to the hull with quick release gear that only takes the pulling of three cotter pins to free them. Mother Nature evidently did not manage to pull the pins, and the violence of the storms we have experienced did not tear them loose. Or perhaps they were ripped free at some time and floated away.

I suspect they are under the forty foot middle section of the hull, which is lying in fifteen feet of water down our shore to the northwest of our camp. Harry saw it, lying upside down at a forty five degree angle, and thought the cylinders might be pinned under it. If that's so, we have no hope of freeing one from the tons of wooden hull resting on them.

Stung by pellets of wind driven rain, knocked about by gusts of wind, and discouraged about the inaccessible canisters, we crawled back inside our shelter, shared an over cooked seagull and a baked egg apiece, and went to sleep.

Love, Grampa

Dear Grandchildren,

A break in the rain! As a result of our excursion this afternoon, our shelter is not going to be as dark as it was a week ago! Why? We are very thankful that we were able to find a two foot piece from the cabin of our boat. The storm apparently broke up our boat even more. There is usually heavy surf which keeps pounding the remains of our vessel. A shattered and ragged edged piece of the cabin washed ashore. We were delighted, and surprised, to find that it contained an unbroken, brass rimmed porthole! As our boat is gradually beaten into ever smaller pieces, we drag ashore any portions that are small enough for the three of us to handle. It was a wooden vessel, as you may recall, and wood burns. With that in mind, we have added some of the smaller pieces of the boat to our little storage nooks inside our shelter, to provide dry wood for fires.

Now that the storm has ended, Harry is working with us to wedge the rough part of the deckhouse, with the porthole in it, into the upper end of our little "summer cottage". If we had any tools to do so, we would remove the porthole from the jagged mess to which it was attached. But as that is not possible, we will create an opening into which we will fit the whole thing. We look forward to the porthole providing light and a limited view of the world outside.

Our work on the porthole project ended before we really got started when a sudden and violent rain shower drove us back into the shelter, as we were not wearing our rain gear when it struck.

You are in my thoughts and prayers, and today, amid this wild wind and violent surf, I hope I am in yours. I pray that you do not give up hope that someday we will be found. But I imagine that, by now, your hope of our safe return is dwindling. If I could somehow communicate to you in spirit, I would ask you to stay hopeful. I know we are working at exactly that!

Today would be a good one for playing family games or watching TV. On the other hand, given our situation here, I think I'll tuck this letter away and take a nap until after supper, when we will venture out again, as the rain seems to be letting up.

Love, Grampa

Dear Grandkids,

The foul weather has diminished in intensity, the rains have stopped. Winds are around twenty miles per hour, and patches of blue sky show themselves occasionally above the dark, scudding clouds.

First thing this morning, we finished the large opening in our shelter and wedged the porthole into position. We weren't quite finished with the project, when the wind picked up and heavy rains returned. So we crawled back inside our shelter and lounged around, listening to the rain and wind, and taking turns at our new, loosely installed "picture window." Not much to see through it, just a limited, water streaked view of the uphill end of our gully, and, when the visibility improves, between the heavier downpours, a bit more of the slope and some sky.

The rain stopped as suddenly as it had begun, so we crawled outside and finished sealing the area around the porthole. That done, our thoughts turned to the next issue facing us.

We have an unpleasant, but necessary chore ahead of us. We have put it off, but decided while we were talking during the storm, that we must stop procrastinating, and act.

All those seals represent a huge amount of meat; and their skins, if we can prepare them somehow, will provide valuable protection from the cold that we know is coming. Harry tells us that he read about seal kills and preparing seal fur. That was years ago when he lived in upper Michigan. We don't know if we can melt down the seal fat for lamp fuel or not. But Melanie reminded us that we need some fat in our diet, and in our bodies, in preparation for winter. Eskimos have known this for thousands of years. I wondered aloud what boiled periwinkles would taste like if dipped in melted seal fat. We are reluctant to kill a seal, mainly because we have become so fond of them, and treasure the experience of walking peacefully among them.

We're not sure how to go about it. We are afraid that trying to slit a seal's throat will put us in physical danger as it thrashes about. And we're not sure how quickly our razor-sharp knife will go through the skin. Also, we are afraid that a wounded seal might lunge for the safety of the ocean and be out of our reach by the time it dies. Well, we've all heard about those baby seal hunts, where hunters club hundreds of them to death. It would seem that clubbing a seal might make more sense.

So we have set about making three club handles from pieces of driftwood. Why make three clubs, you may ask. We do not know if one hit will stun or kill a seal, and we need to be prepared to make multiple strikes if necessary. After all, none of us have ever killed anything. So we concluded, "Better safe than sorry." Hence, the three clubs.

After we shape them and notch them, Harry will bind a rock to the head of each one, using some of the rope we have salvaged from the wreck. He says it may take all day to whittle and shape the three pieces of wood.

Our reluctance to actually engage in the hunt is almost overwhelming. I would guess that we will not get up the courage, and the will to actually do it, for a while. Probably the clubs will sit around and haunt us until we finally get up the courage. We'll see.

I came up with an idea for conserving our Sterno fuel. What if, just before starting a fire, I took a very small blob of Sterno and mixed it with a handful of dried grass and twigs. Would the Sterno/grass mix prove to be a sure and instant fire starter? My companions thought it sounded reasonable, so next time we want to do some cooking, we will give it a try. Also, we will, as we have already done in the past, cook extra amounts of food so that we won't need fire for several days. And we still eat raw eggs, although they are becoming scarce as the season moves on. We also eat clams, or mussels, or whatever they are.

Late this afternoon, as we were sitting on some rocks near the water, I noticed something sort of ghostly undulating slowly beneath the surface, near the shore. I pointed it out to my companions. We stood, changed into our wading footwear, and waded toward it. "Be careful," Harry warned. "We don't know what it is." After looking at it from all sides, we decided it was some sort of white, cloth like stuff. So we waded to it and pulled it toward shore. It turned out to be one of the sails, a jib, from the boat. We figured the storm we just had must have broken the hull up some more, freeing things in the sail locker!

We were ecstatic! The great triangle of nylon sailcloth must be some sixty feet along the long side, and maybe twenty feet at the wide bottom. Not only do we now have virtually indestructible material for our use, but the two long sheets were still attached! The sheets, for your information, are lines that are used to control the jib when it is in use. One is run down each side of the cabin to the cockpit. And, oh happy thought, the sail is fairly water repellant! We'll probably use it to completely cover our somewhat leaky shelter. It should be large enough to cover the shelter and extend across from the door to our shelter to the three sided rock screened firepit. By securing it with rocks and some of the rope we have, we will have a rain and sun roof over our "vacation home" and over the firepit. Seems like a good idea, anyhow, even though I don't have the slightest idea how we might accomplish that. I would hate to have to dismantle the entire shelter! We'll think about it and give it a try soon, I imagine.

I'm thinking of you. My thoughts and prayers go out to you.

Love, Grampa

Dear Family,

It is near dark, and we are totally exhausted. I'll tell you why, and then I'm going to crash!

Our little shelter is very damp, drafty, and cold. I may have mentioned that at some point, but if I didn't, I'm sure you can imagine how chilly the rock walls are, in this cold, damp climate, and with water gurgling along underneath. Melanie wondered if we would possibly put part of the sail under us, on top of the stone floor, and up the rock walls. That set "Harry the Carpenter" to speculating and scratching his head. After a few minutes his expression brightened and he shared his ideas with us.

Here's what we did. We took the sail completely off everything and set it aside, weighted down with rocks, of course, so it wouldn't blow away. Using branches as levers, and removing as few stones and supports as possible from the upper end of the shelter, we began the frustrating process of dragging the bottom edge of the sail under everything and into the shelter. When we had about eight feet of sail inside, in an unwieldy jumble, we rebuilt the upper end of the shelter, leaving the major bulk of the sail outside. After spreading the bottom of the sail over the entire floor, and extending it up the side walls, we returned our bedding and all the other gear and clothes from outdoors. Next we removed as little of the roof as possible so that we could drag and drape the sail up and over the entire structure. We still had ten or fifteen feet of the narrower triangular top of the sail outside our front door. We brought that all the way over the far end of the U-shaped firepit, with enough excess to anchor it very firmly with many rocks. The firepit, by the way, is only a yard from our front door. We wedged and laid branches over all that, tying rope over as much as we could and piling large stones everywhere to anchor the sail and the ropes. I know, this description is not very well written. If I had a computer I would rework it! If I had a camera I could take a picture.

So? The end result is a gully shelter that is totally enclosed on all sides, except the front, counting the rock walls as two of the sides. Our hinged door keeps most of the wind out. And the sail stretches overhead, some three feet above the ground, from our door to the far end of the firepit. And, the really good news is that the firepit is covered, so we can cook and warm ourselves without the inconvenience of rain extinguishing the fire or soaking the firepit, and us in the bargain. If we're not careful we'll have a Class A Resort here before long! Our next project will be to drag and roll rocks to make a windbreak in the three foot space between the west wall of the gully shelter and the west wall of the firepit. I think I may have mentioned that the almost constant wind comes from the west.

I can't really see to write, and my arms are shaking with fatigue. Goodnight!

Love, Grampa

Dear Grandchildren,

This afternoon I realized I have not told you about our usual Sunday morning event.

Unless the weather is really bad, we gather at the top of the knoll at the west end of our island, which is at the opposite end from the cliff, and Spinnaker Rock, as we call it, for our regular "Island Wide Interfaith Worship Service." Everyone on the island takes part! As I may have mentioned, our religious backgrounds are different: Harry was brought up Roman Catholic, Melanie's father was Jewish, and I, as you know, was brought up in various church traditions – Baptist, Congregational, and Methodist.

The service itself is quite simple. First we sit in silence, looking out to sea, or more often than not, staring into the fog, one of us facing west, one east, and one south. We spend that time meditating within ourselves, focusing on good things either here on the island, or far, far away where our loved ones are. Then we stand, face each other, and hold hands to recite the Lord's Prayer and sing the Doxology. It would sound strange, were there anyone to hear the words floating across the top of an uninhabited island: "Praise God from whom all blessings flow, praise him all creatures here below." We're not exactly the Mormon Tabernacle Choir, but, who's to hear us and complain? After our brief service, we usually sit facing south together and one of us may recite words from our religious literature, from memory, of course, as we have no books, or we share a poem or other memorized bit of inspiration.

Finally, to avoid the possibility of getting depressed if we slip into thinking about our predicament and how much we miss our loved ones, we stand up and hike back to our shelter for lunch, which we have named our "Island Wide Interfaith Potluck Dinner."

Thought for the day? Humor is important in life. Don't ever lose your sense of humor! And never laugh <u>at</u> anyone, only <u>with</u> that person. We have found here on our island prison, that humor often alleviates our depression!

Our dread about our seal kill distracted us from the results of the storm, as did the Sunday religious service. This afternoon Harry broached the subject of the canisters again. He wondered if the heavy surf might have shifted the large section of hull that had them trapped. So we walked along the shore at low tide, looking for them. At low tide we could sometimes see the deep keel poking up near the surface, slightly awash in the waves. We got kind of excited when we could not see it. "Maybe it finished rolling over?" Melanie remarked hopefully.

"I'm diving for it tomorrow!" Harry insisted. Try as we might, we have not been able to talk him out of it. So tomorrow we will go to the spot where it should be and Harry will make one dive. He promised he would not go down more than twice, in order to avoid the hypothermia that almost killed him the last time he dove.

Love, Grampa

Well, dear grandchildren,

Harry made his dive just before lunch. Just as we hoped, the hull had rolled, partially anyhow. Now it rests in maybe twenty feet of water, "on its side," he shouted to us. That was the good news. But he was not happy. That was obvious to us standing waist deep near the shore. But he said nothing and disappeared under the small waves for a second time. When he came up, he swam ashore to us, regained his breath, and told us the bad news: the canister on what was now the upper side was badly crushed. He had checked the cotter pin release mechanisms, and found two of them so badly bent that there was no way he could pull the cotter pins without tools, like a pair of vise grips. Our spirits were crushed by the news. But we walked away from our despair and boiled a large pot of periwinkles for lunch. That buoyed our spirits somewhat and our afternoon walk brought us back to our usual cheerful selves. I should note that Harry lived to tell the tale of his ice water swim with nothing more than a half hour of intense shivering and a strong desire for some hot seaweed tea.

So? When things look bad, walk away and do something to get back on track. Standing around moping gets you nowhere! Play catch, vacuum the living room, wash the car, go for a run, go to a movie, but do <u>something</u> to help take your mind off your failure, or your mistake, or your misfortune.

I leave you with that.

Love, Grampa

Dear Grandkids,

This morning Harry asked, "Do you think we'll die here?" His comment, while violating our agreed-upon optimistic mindset, was not to be taken lightly. After all we do need to talk through our doubts and fears.

Melanie's answer was simple and to the point, "I sure as Hell hope not! We're already in Hell, are we not?" We chuckled for a moment, then decided to hike up to the high point of our island and have a talk. We wanted to have this discussion well away from our shelter area, for we have long ago decided to hash out any serious "negative topics" far enough away that they will not haunt our daily routine. Does that make sense to you? We don't want any gloomy emotional clouds hanging about where we spend our time. There are enough real clouds and fog in the air as it is! Ha ha!

That was late this morning. Now, having done our forage walk, which grows increasingly more difficult, we are settled in to write letters before supper, as it is drizzly and foggy. Harry netted an eighteen inch fish of some sort just after lunch. It got itself into a pool among the rocks and didn't leave soon enough. The tide went out and left it stranded! So tonight we will build a fire in our covered firepit out front and bake the fish, steam a big pot of periwinkles for tomorrow's lunch, and try to net a gull or two and cook them in the coals for tomorrow also. Oh boy, fish for dinner!

So, dear ones, what about death? What's next? Anything?

Let me start with the obvious: Few of us want to die. There are exceptions, of course. People in severe pain (physical, spiritual, or emotional) may experience such despair that they no longer have anything to live for. They would rather die than continue in their present state.

I do not know what comes next, and neither do you! "Now we see though a glass darkly." We would like to be able to clean that glass and see clearly. So we speculate, wonder, question, pray, and hope. The results of all that wondering are so diverse we can barely comprehend the variety.

Here's a partial list of "possibilities." Melanie, Harry and I came up with it when were up on the "mountain" this morning having our discussion about death. Life after death possibilities: 1/ Sitting at the right hand of God. 2/ Being reunited with loved ones who have died before us. 3/ Returning to earth reincarnated. 4/ Sitting on a cloud with a harp, making music. 5/ Living in a mansion ("In my Father's house are many mansions."). 6/ Enjoying the delights of many virgins. 7/ Feeling the weight and pain of eternal damnation. 8/ Flying about with wings as eagles. 9/ Lying there waiting for the resurrection to come someday. 10/ Existing in a common spiritual state of some sort. 11/ Wandering this earth invisible and silent. 12/

Absolute nothingness. 13/ Singing in a heavenly choir. 14/ Being reborn in some other life, free of physical and mental handicaps. 15/ "Going" somewhere. 16/ "Being" something. 16/ Joining in a vast spiritual Being. 17/ Remaining, somehow, in God's eternal care. 18/ Reliving our total experience and the experiences others had of us. 19/ Etc.

Atheists laugh at our wishful thinking, insisting that all "religious views" are nothing more than a crutch, some sort of "comfort food" for our souls.

Agnostics simply leave it that "I don't know, and I'll find out when I die." Maybe the agnostic view is good enough for you. I hope it is not. As for me, I need something more.

One of my favorite ways of looking at all this is known as "Pascal's Wager." Blaise Pascal was a philosopher back in the past. Quite simply it goes like this: 1/ There is no GOD, with "God" including life beyond the grave, and I believe that, 2/ There is no GOD but I believe there is one, 3/ There is a GOD but I don't believe that is true, and 4/ There is a GOD and I believe that.

Rather than "preach a little sermon" here on the topic, let me urge you to play with Pascal's options for a while. Imagine the outcome of believing any one of them. I can predict what will probably happen within you: You will come to realize that the second and fourth choices make the most sense for coping with death and dying in a meaningful way. The first choice leads to despair, or maybe into a kind of Stoicism, and the third choice has the same result. So, run with this, my dear grandchildren. See where it leads you. I hope and pray the result will be a decision to live as if God and life after death both exist!

Love, Grampa

Dear Grandkids,

We are a bit depressed today. I'll explain in a moment. But first...

As we come to accept the possibility that we may die here, we have found parts of the 23rd Psalm increasingly comforting. Sometimes we recite them together. "The Lord is my shepherd, I shall not want." At that point in our recitation, we sometimes glance at each other, grin, and roll our eyes, for we are facing hunger, foul weather, and a terribly uncertain future.

"He leadeth me beside the still waters." Here we look toward the restless and often wild surf, when we can see it through the fog. "Yeah, right", Melanie might comment.

After a pause, we often join hands and say together, "Yea though I walk through the valley of the shadow of death I will fear no evil; for Thou art with me." Sometimes the words feel hollow, empty, meaningless. At other times they almost bring tears of joy. This is hard to explain to you. We are in a desperate situation, but we have faith that, even if we die here, we are in God's care. Don't take this in any trivial way, kids. When life looks bleak, or your spirit is depressed, there is a huge comfort in feeling that you are not alone. As the 23rd Psalm also says, "He restoreth my soul." Strangely, that is true!

Now let me tell you why we are especially down today.

I write this with a heavy heart. Today is gloomy, moderately foggy, damp, cool and depressing, fitting weather for our mood. We have decided that tomorrow we are going to go kill a seal. The gulls no longer provide eggs for us, and we <u>must</u> save our canned goods for winter. We have no source, other than the seals, for meat, fat, or warm skins with which to cover ourselves when winter gets here. We have to do it, but we hate it!

I am too upset to write more today.

I love you all so much, and miss you!

Love, Grampa

Dear Grandkids,

I love you and miss you.

Today was as bad as we feared it would be. After a long restless night of little sleep, we arose, forced ourselves to eat a light breakfast, went for our hike, moved a few large rocks from the pathway, and dragged some driftwood to our campsite. We got a small fire started for use later. Finally, by mid morning, realizing we were putting off what we had to do, we gathered our clubs, the big army knife, some rope for hauling the dead seal, and trudged, with heavy hearts, toward the seal colony.

We wandered among the animals for a while, looking for our "victim." When Harry thus referred to our future target, we laughed, but our laughs were thin and empty of humor. It was Melanie who spotted an injured seal at the seaward edge of the colony. It had a mangled flipper and several deep gashes on its body near the distorted and bloody appendage. We surmised it must have escaped from a predator of some sort, perhaps a killer whale. Our planned killing now also became a matter of euthanizing an injured seal. But that didn't provide much comfort for us.

I'm not sure how much of the gory details to put down on paper. So, with apologies for what I will write, here goes.

We slowly approached the wounded seal, then spent some time with it, talking softly as we approached and stood beside it, Harry to the right, me to its left, and Melanie in front of it. I was shaking, and Melanie was crying softly by the time Harry nodded and we raised our clubs. As prearranged, Harry was the first to hit the seal's head as hard as he could. As it emitted a strange sort of screech, I hit it from my position on its left. It collapsed, and lay motionless. Melanie, per our agreement to <u>all</u> take part in the tragedy; struck with her club. Then she set her weapon aside, knelt and put her face near its nostrils. "He's not breathing," she whispered. In a tender, spontaneous gesture, we placed our hands on its motionless body and bowed our heads for several seconds.

"Okay, let's get on with it," said Harry softly. We tied our length of rope around its tail fins, picked up our bloody Stone Age clubs, grasped the rope firmly and began the difficult task of dragging the carcass away from the herd. Once we had "him" well away from the others, we stopped below the high tide line, arranged the body on a ragged four foot square of warped plywood and began the process of "dressing" it. Why eviscerating, skinning and butchering is called "dressing" makes no sense to us. It was a sad, but, of course necessary, chore.

Melanie and Harry were hard at work, while I went to our campsite and added wood to the fire we had left.

By the time we had clumsily removed the bulk of its skin and emptied the abdominal cavity, our grieving was just about over, and we worked with more enthusiasm as we celebrated, if that is the right word, the meat and hide that was now part of our survival. I commented, "I hope we don't have to do this again for a long time, maybe never." There were no arguments against that, I can assure you! A large number of seagulls gathered in a raucous flurry to dive and fight over the entrails.

Melanie added a hopeful note when she looked up, hands bloodied from cutting meat into thin strips, and said, "Hopefully we'll be rescued before the need arises again." Melanie was pretty good at cutting the meat away from the bones and getting it ready for cooking. Harry helped her when he could and began the chore of scraping the inside of the seal's skin, gradually removing fat and tissue. We used our knife and clamshell halves to do the scraping. Each pass with the edge of a shell netted only a small bit of tissue. This is going to be a long, difficult, and painful, process. We'll need many breaks, as the job is really hard on our hands.

I drew the task of lugging the head, flippers, and what remained of the organs down to the shore at the western end of the island, and throwing them as far out to sea as I could, in the hope that something would eat them. We certainly had no thought of doing so!

By midafternoon we had brought the meat, bones and skin to our campsite. The large fire had died down somewhat. We tossed the larger bones into the fire, hoping we would be able to later crack them and eat the marrow, which we believed would be nutritious. The meat was wrapped in layers of seaweed, mostly kelp, and also placed in the coals. We cut chunks of fat into pieces that would fit in the cooking pot and put it over the fire to "render," as Melanie called it.

While we sat by the fire we talked. "I wonder if seals have souls," Harry muttered to himself. "I used to ask myself that about my dogs when they died."

At that, both of them turned their heads in my direction. Melanie smirked, asked, "What do you think, Chaplain?"

"I think I don't know, but it's easy to imagine that God cares for all his creatures. There is that thing in the Bible about "not a sparrow falls." So why wouldn't it be possible?"

We tossed that around for a while. After a few minutes of silence, it dawned on me that this might be something of interest to you, my grandchildren. So I excused myself, got my writing stuff from inside the shelter and seated myself on a rock nearby.

So let me recommend this thought to you: I believe there is a spirit world, which "surrounds" us. I can't decide what words best describe an indwelling spiritual reality, so I use the word surrounds. I remember that one of you, many years ago, asked me if I believed in ghosts. If you remember, I said that I did. If there is a spirit world, it must be kind of like a "parallel universe" that science fiction writers sometimes write about. And if that is possible, and ghosts, or spirits, of people who have died live on somehow, then where does that lead us? I believe that we are always in God's care. I don't know what that will be like after I die, but I trust in it; I believe in it; I hope for it. And if that kind of thing is true, why, then our lives make more sense. Give it a lot of thought, please. What you come up with, what you hope is true, will shape your life, for better or for worse!

Whether or not you will ever read these words is not up to me. I hope fate decrees that you see these letters. And of course I hope I live to give them to you!

I love you, all of you: my beloved wife, my wonderful children and your spouses, and you, my precious grandchildren.

Love, Grampa

Dear Grandkids,

Well, we finished our cooking task last Saturday and had our first taste of seal meat. It was delicious! Remember, we are gradually losing weight as we slowly seem to be starving. And we have had no red meat since before mid June. It rejuvenated us! We even drank some of the hot seal oil, not a pleasant thing, but Melanie insisted, saying we needed some fat in our diet. It gave us hope that we might last through the winter.

Harry brought out the bag of rock salt and we ground it into a fine texture before applying it to the raw side of the sealskin, which we have scraped and scraped and scraped. We think we should scrape it and salt it several times. Then, as Melanie instructed us, we need to do what all primitive cultures did with an animal skin: knead it, bend it, and fold it to make it supple. Don't know if it will work, but we plan on working the sealskin like that for several more days. It's beginning to stink a bit, but it will provide warmth someday when we need it. We agree that warmth and survival trumps stink and unpleasantness!

Now for an abrupt change of subject: We had been chatting, and after a while had concluded that lust for power, or greed, was perhaps the root of all evil. We all want to have control over our lives; we don't like it when control is taken out of our hands. That's what has happened to us shipwrecked survivors, isn't it? We have lost much of the control of our destinies. We agreed with the old saying that "power corrupts and absolute power corrupts absolutely." I hope you will keep that in mind as you grow strong, gain promotions at work, or find friends listening attentively to any "words of wisdom" you might be emitting.

The three of us switched to talking about clergy and the power they wield over their parishoners when it comes to guiding them to save their eternal souls. Actually we started out discussing politicians, military commanders, kings, corporate executives, and presidents, the power they wield, and the ways they often abuse it. I got the bright idea of turning the discussion toward religious leaders. I declared that ministers, priests, and rabbis can be caught up in a feeling of power that leads them toward pride and away from humility. When it is claimed that "I, being a clergyperson, know more than you do about God's intentions and about life after death," we are victims of our own worst enemy: pride in the power our faith leadership gives us. After all, what is more powerful than being able to tell people about the next life, about Eternity?

My advice to you, kids, is this: beware of the danger of the power trap! I must add that, as a chaplain, I never felt that my position as a minister gave me the right to claim any sort of "Absolute Knowledge." It was my job, I believed, and I still do, to share ideas and possibilities in such a way that my congregation and counselees might internalize what I've offered and "work

Donald G. Vedeler

it over" for themselves. I sometimes distrust the motives of people who claim authoritative knowledge on subjects that are as nebulous and unprovable as religious subjects are!

Love, Grampa

Dear Grandchildren,

We had an interesting discussion last night, which lasted into the wee hours of the morning. Lying there in our pitch dark shelter, we got to talking about the idea of accepting Jesus as your one and only Lord and Savior. We shared religious ideas and experiences from our pasts, and concluded that many, many people, including neighbors, relatives, friends, community leaders, and even some strangers who touched our lives briefly, influenced us for the better. Melanie, half jokingly, suggested it might be more accurate to talk about our Lords and Saviors!

Well, let me tell you: her putting an S on the words stopped us in our tracks. And then we were off again, discovering and rediscovering hundreds of events, people, dramatic productions, and books that led us, directed us for the better, and saved us from mistakes that might have been.

So, precious grandkids, pull up a chair and read on. I fantasize that I will survive this isolation, make my way home, and go to a copy center to replicate a separate set of these letters for each of you! Here's what I have to offer today. You have been, and will be, influenced again and again by forces outside yourself. Some of them will change you for the better; some for the worse. It is up to you not only to choose, but to consciously pull the good ones inside, internalize them; make them part of you, and allow them to "save" you.

I have been "saved" by the love and wisdom of my parents, the warm ministry of the pastor of one church I attended as a teenager, two high school teachers, and my college track coach. Need I go on? I'm sure you get the point. I have also been "saved" by books I have read, or parts of them anyway. In particular I have been "saved" by reading the words of Martin Luther, St. Augustine, and Plato! I have been saved, or partially led toward salvation, by deeply moving parts of movies, plays, or hymns sung in church.

It boils down to this: salvation, whatever that is, is not usually the result of accepting Jesus, or Mohammed, or Moses, as a one and only savior. Rather, Jesus is one savior among many. Most of us have been influenced, for the better, by someone other than Jesus of Nazareth. In fact, the depth and power of those influences often outweighs by far the influence of Jesus in our lives.

To put it differently: God reaches into our lives to help, guide, strengthen, and influence us in many ways. Don't put a harness on Him. Do not try to limit the subtle and not so subtle times, places, and ways He works! Melanie, Harry and I came to the rather startling conclusion that it may be a serious mistake to lean on one "Savior" to the exclusion of others! It is the grace of God, not the touch of any one "Savoir" that will lead us Home.

Donald G. Vedeler

If you lean in this direction with your beliefs, you will also open the door of your heart to people of faith who adhere to another Book, or another Savior, or another creed. "God works in wondrous ways."

Love, Grampa

Dear Grandkids,

We spent the entire morning walking the perimeter of our island. Harry suggested that we take such a shoreline walk. He recalled seeing lobster pots near shore, while on vacation in Maine years ago. Last night he asked, "Is it possible that there are lobstermen living on nearby islands?" So we scanned the nearby waters with great care, high hopes, and a dash of skepticism.

But his suggestion turned out to be a good one, because, late in the morning, as we clambered among the rocks, and walked the short sandy beaches on the northwest shore, we were stopped in our tracks by the sight of something floating about 75 yards off shore. Melanie clambered up on a partially submerged boulder, and confirmed that it was a yellow and white buoy! Some distance beyond it to the east was a second matching one. "Don't lobster fishermen usually run several traps with a marker buoy at each end?" she shouted.

"Yes. Yes, I believe they do," Harry replied.

Needless to say, we were astounded. And again we asked ourselves, "Why haven't we been looking for these for weeks?" I sometimes wonder what kind of survivors we are, when we didn't even think to do this. We might have spotted a lobster boat and been rescued if we had happened along this stretch of shore at the right time. I wanted to ask Harry why he had not brought the business of lobster traps up sooner. But I didn't. To do so would have served no useful purpose other than to make Harry feel guilty.

I got to thinking about that; and The Golden Rule popped to mind. "Do unto others as you would have them do unto you." I certainly would not want Melanie or Harry to dig at me for things I had not thought to mention. We have enough to worry about here without dropping recriminations on each other's shoulders.

And so, dear grandchildren, I offer this to you: Before you say or do something that might offend or hurt another person, count to ten and ask if what you are contemplating will serve any useful purpose. Ask yourself, "Would I want someone to do this, or say this, to me?"

The Golden Rule is, to my way of thinking, one of the most loving and valuable guides we have. All this ties in with things I've written earlier, so I won't belabor it here. But I will make one suggestion. When you wake up in the morning, say the Golden Rule to yourself before you start your day. It will enrich your relationships and avoid putting burdens on your conscience when you fail to live by it because you forgot about it!

I can't believe we have been here more than two months! And, yes, I sink into despair at times. But the agreement the three of us made to stay positive prevents me from dwelling on my downcast moods or sharing them with my companions. We are allowed to simply mention it when we feel depressed, and then talk about something else. Changing the subject from depression to something different, makes it possible for the other two to try to buoy the spirits of the one who is feeling down. Speaking of which, namely buoys, we will, from now on, make an effort to climb to the top of our island and scan the seas in all directions. Well, when the fog is not present, anyway.

Will we be looking when the lobsterman comes to check or remove his line of traps? I pray that we will!

Love, Grampa

Dear Grandchildren,

It should come as no surprise that we are weakening as the weeks pass. We find the effort of moving boulders and rocks, climbing up slopes, and foraging, gets more and more tiring. Our clothes hang loose. We are losing weight. Fortunately our general health remains very good: no sickness, nor injuries. This deterioration is not good, but it is to be expected, of course. We'll continue to deal with it, and as they say, "hope for the best, anticipate the worst, and take what comes." I wonder how much worse off we would be if we had not begun our adventure in excellent physical condition (for our ages, that is!).

Yesterday Melanie was fretting about her decision to go on this Adventure Cruise. "Why did I ever decide to put myself at risk on an adventure like this?" she asked, speaking aloud as we walked along the south shore. Good question!

As we walked, I recalled the words of a philosophy professor in college who spent an hour talking about gambling. He defined gambling as "unnecessarily putting values at risk." He stressed the word, "unnecessarily." He went on to point out that risk is a part of human existence, a necessary part. I volunteered to be an army chaplain years ago, knowing that I ran the risk of being sent to Vietnam. But, I did it because I wanted to serve my fellow man, and, I told myself, I wished to serve God. That kind of thing, our professor stated, was not gambling. "Values," we were told, included virtually everything, particularly money, health, and friendships. He pointed out that "recreational" gambling was not a good thing, because to put values like those at risk unnecessarily detracts from life's goal of living meaningful, loving, circumspect lives.

Of course, when Melanie, Harry, and I had this discussion, we talked about compulsive gamblers who dream of getting rich at casinos. We also talked about friends we have known who drove recklessly, skied like mad fools, or in other ways sought excitement through taking risks for the fun of it.

By now you can see what's coming: another piece of wise advice from your Grampa Gregg. Take risks when they might make the world a better place. Avoid taking risks when they are attempts at finding an easy way out, merely thrill seeking, or gambling values unnecessarily. However, I admit that I have taken unnecessary risks at times in my life. I can think of a few times behind the wheel of my parents' car, and I am lucky nothing bad came of them. I recognize that the spirit of adventure often makes life sing a joyful song. However: think it through first, before you take risks. No one wants to be a boring Casper Milquetoast. But no one wants to be a crippled or dead person either. "Look before you leap," is good advice. To put it another way, be sure there are no rocks hidden under the surface before you dive in. Be sure the water is deep enough. Yada, yada, yada. I'm sure you get the drift.

Donald G. Vedeler

   If I ever get to come home to all of you, I don't want to find one of you dead, homeless, or in a wheelchair because you gambled!
   I love you!

Love, Grampa

Dearest Grandchildren,

Today was a bad one! Our food supply is getting low and we have not had any meat, neither seagulls nor seals, for more than a week. The seal meat has spoiled. Nurse Melanie insisted it was <u>that</u> time again; we had put it off as long as we could. Our health requirements demand it. So now it was time to kill another seal! So, we gathered our clubs and carcass dressing instruments and headed for the seal colony.

We walked among our big eyed friends with heavy hearts. We spent two hours wandering among them, and finally found what we had hoped, with little optimism, to find: another injured seal. His left flipper was badly torn and bent at an impossible angle. A huge gash ran half the length of his side. Its left eye was destroyed and bloody. S/he was barely above the waves, indicating to us that s/he could not easily get any farther up the rocky shore. We don't know how to tell males from females, so from now on I'll simply refer to them as males.

So we killed it. And it tore at our hearts to do so. As before, after it was dead, we stood holding hands and asking forgiveness for taking its life. It is easy to understand why many "primitive" hunters do that sort of thing. It made us feel a little bit better. Hunting for survival is not the same as hunting for sport, but killing still hurts us when we have to do it. I'm sure that any hunter to whom we might tell this, would shake his head and scoff.

I have not mentioned the other seal skin. We have worked it and worked it and salted it one more time, and scraped it again and again. It still smells, but, lying under it with the fur against us is warm, warm, warm. We have again salted it, rolled it tightly, and tied it with a bit of ship's line. When winter really gets here, but hoping we are not here when it does, we know our survival is more likely, thanks to the sealskin.

Back to the carcass: as before, we dressed the seal, and cooked everything we might eat. We had started a fire before we set out on our hunt. We have, in the past, used the blubber like cooking oil to keep meat and fish and seagull meat from sticking to that precious iron skillet. It works, and the taste is not as repugnant now as it was at first. If it's good enough for Eskimos, it's good enough for us! Maybe we'll regain some of the weight we have lost?

This must be upsetting for you to read, if you are in fact reading it, if we have in fact survived, or if our remains have been found along with these letters.

Sometimes I wonder why I bother writing these letters. Who will ever see them? But it helps maintain sanity and hope. You may have noted that my letter writing is becoming less frequent, less regular. I should probably jot things down. But there is a sameness to each day such that is not worth putting the details down on paper: frequent fog, strong winds, persistent rains, increasingly chilly air, and those rare, welcome, warmer, sunny days, and all the repetitive daily walks: scrounging and hunting for food, and scanning around our island for boats that never seem to come, chewing on various plant items, and our personal hygiene activities. We are not as strong as we were, and hard work, like climbing to Spinnaker Rock, seems to tire us out. We just don't have the energy we had. This is a bit discouraging, of course. But we will continue to do the best we can with the situation we have been handed.

Dear God, guide <u>someone</u> to find us!

Love, Grampa

Dear Grandchildren,

We took our last "baths" today, as the air temperatures have been dropping steadily for the past two weeks. My guess is that we rarely are going to see anything above 50° from now on. So we took advantage of the sunny, breezy day that was offered to us today. It is just too cold to strip down and clean ourselves. So we'll have to endure the lice that now share our clothing and bedding with us. Did I mention that we have gradually become infested with them?

As you probably have figured out by now, our Island Paradise is mostly cold, windy, rainy and foggy. Sometimes the fog is so thick we cannot see ten feet. At other times it is thin enough that we can see most of our island. Sometimes it comes in bunches, wisps of thick fog interspersed with patches of hazy sun, occasionally even a glimpse of faded blue sky overhead. Hanging over all this is the fear that we will never be able to escape from this place.

We are trapped in a nightmare from which we are unable to wake up. Melanie called our predicament "an adventure dream turned nightmare."

"We dreamed of adventure, signed up, and here we are," Harry added, with a grimace.

Which led us to talk about doing things you "always wanted to do."

Follow your dream, anything you would like to accomplish in life, even if it is simply for your own satisfaction. We all have good things we want to do. I qualify it with the word "good," because if it is likely to cause pain to others, or make the world a worse place, then recognize it as a nightmare and discard it. If you have a dream of wielding power over others, or getting rich at the expense of others, or being dishonest about something, forget it, reject it!

I had always wanted to go on some big adventure. And I did. Here I am in a terrible predicament, but it came as a result of having the courage, if you will, to reach out for the "brass ring", an expression from the merry-go-round days, and to follow a dream. Hiking on the Mendenhall Glacier in Alaska was one such dream and it felt good, real good, to fulfill it. At this point I'm not sure the risk was worth it, but we shall see what the future brings before we pass judgment on that! A friend took up the trumpet after thirty some years of not playing. With practice and enthusiasm he has exceeded his former skill and enjoys playing in local bands. Another friend, in spite of painful and debilitating chronic illness, is writing a book about triumph over the tragedy of chronic illness, another dream being achieved, despite only being able to work on the book for a half hour or less at a time. I have an army chaplain friend who dreamed of writing a novel. After hard work and much enjoyment he has two books in print.

You may be too busy now. And later when you have a spouse and family and job to take up your time, talents, and energy, well, you might have to put your dream "on hold" for a while. But when the opportunity comes? <u>Follow your dream!</u>

Now back to the matter of our life here in paradise. We continue to cross the island to look for that fishing boat that we missed a while back. Also, above the high tide line on the sandy beaches are two plants that we use for food. One is some sort of grain, whether wheat, barley or oats, we don't know. We have meticulously harvested the seeds at the top of each plant. We once tried to crush the grains in a rock hollow to get rid of the husks and grind them into a powder, hoping to create some sort of flat pan bread. But the incessant winds blew the husk and the grains away. So we boil the grains, with the husks, and eat them that way. Tomorrow we will drag a concave rock inside our shelter and try stripping the outer husks by gently grinding them in the depression with a smaller rock. We experimented with the other plant, finding that the leaves have kind of a bitter citrus flavor. So we boil them and make a kind of soup, pretending we are in the tropics enjoying a warm, tropical cocktail.

When things aren't exactly as you wish they were, use your imagination to make them seem better than they really are. Maybe this is one secret to happiness? Maybe poor and destitute folks on farms, in primitive rural shacks, and in slums do this habitually? It works for us, somewhat.

I miss you all so very, very much!

Love, Grampa

Dear Ones,

Today we wandered around in the fog, climbed to Spinnaker Rock and stacked more rocks on the sail, as winds have shaken a corner loose and we fear it will shred. Then we went to our "Church." Harry once called it "The Church of the Holy Castaways." There we hold our Island Wide Ecumenical Service.

For lunch we choked down some dry seaweed, nibbled on some of the little clover like plants we found up in the one hundred square yard depression at the middle of our island, and, literally, "chewed the fat". Melanie has made a mix of tiny strips of cooked seal meat and seal fat, which she believes will help us retain weight. Who ever thought eating fat would be a "health measure?"

A couple of days ago I curled up in the lee of a boulder and drew a little map of our island. It was something to do, a boredom reliever of sorts. The map has twenty foot contour lines to show the shape and elevations. It should be fairly accurate, as Harry looked it over and made suggestions. He has a pretty accurate "carpenter's eye" for distances and heights. Today I redid it and then drew a profile view of the island based on the map. Harry showed me how to do that. Harry knows how to use trigonometry to estimate heights, and in our case, land elevations. The little map gives us all a sense of perspective about our island home and will be comforting to look at when the all too common fog rolls in and we can't see ten feet! Maybe someday we will be rescued and I will be able to give you a graphic idea of our island. We make choices that will either improve our morale or degrade it. This little map gave our spirits a tiny boost upward.

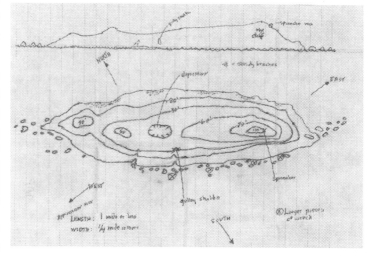

I may have mentioned this before: have you given much thought to the choices you make each day? They often seem unimportant, these daily decisions. But who knows? I had a seminary professor who talked about the "ISness of the WAS." His point? Our past is always with us. So when we decide to do good or smart things, we build habits and memories that make us feel good about ourselves. But there is a dark side to "the WAS." When we do stupid, ill advised, or hurtful things, they also live within us as time goes by, making us think a little less of ourselves, and sometimes building "bad" habits that become harder and harder to shake as we live by them. So? Look before you leap, think before you act. Consider what long term results may come from what you are thinking about doing. Overcoming the despair or our past mistakes can be daunting and difficult. I have struggled for years with this. "I have done those things which I ought not to have done, and I have left undone those things which I ought to have done." So, duh, why not "do it right the first time" and avoid the regrets later?

As I've suggested before when I try to make an important point about living: think about it!

Love, Grampa

DAY 74
Sunday, September 10th, 2006

Dear Ones,

Today we wandered around in the fog, climbed to Spinnaker Rock and stacked more rocks on the sail, as winds have shaken a down-wind corner loose and we fear it will shred. Then we went to our "Church" (Harry once called it "The Church of the Holy Castaways,") for our Island-Wide Ecumenical Service, For lunch we choked down some dry seaweed, nibbled on some of the little clover-like plants we found up in the 100-yard depression at the middle of our island, and (literally) "chewed the fat". Melanie has made a mix of tiny strips of cooked seal meat and seal fat, which she believes will help us retain weight. Who ever thought eating fat would be a "health measure?"

A couple of days ago I curled up in the lee of a boulder and drew a little map of our island. It was something to do, a boredom reliever of sorts. The map has 20-foot contour lines to show the shape and elevations. It should be fairly accurate, as Harry looked it over and made suggestions. He has a pretty accurate "carpenter's eye" for distances and heights. Today I re-did it and then drew a profile of the island based on the map (Harry showed me how to do that.) Harry knows how to use trigonometry to estimate heights... and in our case, land elevations. The little map gives us all a sense of perspective about our island home and will be comforting to look at when the all-too-common fog rolls in and we can't see ten feet! Maybe someday we will be rescued and I will be able to give you a graphic idea of our island. We make choices that will

75

Dear Grandkids,

You may be grownups by the time you read this.

The fog lifted yesterday! I guess I should be recording the weather conditions each time I write, for posterity, if there is one?

So we made it a point to walk the high ground repeatedly and scan the horizon for a boat. Day after day, when it is clear, we do this, but to no avail. A couple of times we might see a tiny speck on the horizon, when we can see the horizon, that is, but it never comes closer, just inches ever so slowly along and then it is gone.

But not today!! Today, around noon, we spotted a boat speck. As it gradually became larger, we began to hope it would continue in our direction. So we lit the signal fire, and, once it was burning intensely, threw seaweed on it. The yellowish smoke cloud rose in the nearly still air, a huge "column of hope!" As we watched, we realized that the boat was traveling at an oblique angle to our island. It got slightly closer, and our hopes rose. Then it was no longer coming closer; it gradually began to diminish in size. We shouted at it, although it was probably six miles or so off.

There was no visible response, no change of course.

The boat gradually got tiny, then disappeared.

There are no words to convey our despair. We sat, shoulder to shoulder on a large rock near the dying fire, and our very souls seemed to die inside us. Melanie cried softly; Harry cursed under his breath, and I just sat there staring into space. After about twenty minutes, Melanie wiped her face with her sleeve, got up and said, "Okay. That's it: enough wallowing in self-pity, time to go have a bite to eat and rebuild our signal fire for next time." She was right of course, and, realizing that, Harry and I got to our feet and followed her back to our shelter.

"There are boats out there," I said, "and maybe someday one will see us."

Melanie remarked that all our signal smoke reminded her of smoking and people who smoke. "Stupid," she commented, "Just plain stupid!" That led me to thinking about you, my six dear grandchildren. I hope you never started smoking, but if you have please, for the sake of your health and longevity, quit! What I am about to write may sound harsh, but here goes anyway. With all the medical knowledge at our fingertips today, young people (teens through thirties) are <u>stupid</u> if they choose to smoke, or chew tobacco. Yes, I used the word "stupid!" There is no justification for it, unless you want to include rebellion against parents and adults, or some sort of expression of independence, thumbing noses at adults and their wisdom. I don't know what else might motivate young men and women to take up smoking. Melanie and I, in our respective professional capacities as nurse and chaplain, have stood by and watched people die because they smoked, and tried to comfort their loved ones as they grieved. So many illnesses arise, in part from smoking. All that unnecessary suffering and grieving, and for what? So some idiot could smoke themselves to death! I love you all. Do not smoke!

Change of subject: We have seen many bushes on the west end of the island that seem to be wild roses, the kind you see along northern beaches in New England. So what, you ask? Well, after the blossoms fall off they form a tiny fruit that gradually grows to about small plum size and turns bright red orange. I had heard they were edible, and we have been waiting for them to ripen, as we don't want to waste them by finding them bitter and inedible. Also we want to let them grow to their maximum size, more food, you see.

Well today we picked one and tasted it. Not too bitter, so we each ate one and left for our shelter to see if we would experience stomach cramps or any other unpleasant digestive reactions. Good news: we felt no ill after effects! So we have a new food source.

That good news helped improve our morale after the heartbreaking boat episode.

So, here we are, at the end of our seventy-seventh day here, regaining our sometimes faked optimism, and watching the sun set behind us to our right rear. Tomorrow will be another day, and our message to ourselves this evening is: never give up hope! I pray that you have not given up hope, about me, or about your own lives and any difficulties you may encounter.

Oh, how I miss you!

Love, Grampa

Dear Ones,

Today at our Island Wide Ecumenical Service, Melanie teased Harry about his "religious expletives" that he uttered when that boat did not see us last Wednesday. That led us to a discussion of "taking the Lord's name in vain." Here's the gist of it, tailored to my beloved grandchildren, whatever your age by the time you read this.

I was brought up believing that if I used "God" or "Jesus Christ" as an expletive, I was being naughty. In some religions you are not even supposed to say God's name, even in worship! But let's ignore that for now. Clergy I have known insist that the commandment, "thou shalt not take the name of the Lord thy God in vain" means not to use any references to God or Jesus in a "cussing" manner. Over the years I have come to believe that "taking the Lord's name in vain" is an entirely different matter. So here goes

When religious people, clergy in particular, claim that they know what God wants, are they not being vain in their thinking that <u>they</u> know what <u>God</u> wants? I know: they often use the Bible as their "excuse" saying it is God's Word, and therefore, whenever they say "God wants" they base it on the Bible. But I have already written about that, about how we choose our sacred writings and decide that they are God's literal Word. Is it not vanity to believe and/or claim that we can possibly know what God wants? "God wants us to tithe." God wants me to stop bickering with my sister." "God doesn't want you to do that!" "God wants us to be baptized." "God wants us to be baptized by immersion." You get the idea, don't you? Who am I to tell someone else what God wants him or her to do?

We frail humans cannot possibly begin to comprehend or know who God is or what God wants. We can only guess. We have no words in our language to name God, to describe the spirit world, or to tell others about the deep inner workings of God's spirit in our individual psyches! I am convinced that God wants us to love our neighbors as ourselves. I hope I'm right. But I have no proof that God, whatever "God" is, wants that love to come in the form of converting others to <u>my</u> beliefs, or even to visit the sick and feed the poor. Maybe God wants us to kill bad people, I don't know. That's the key: I/we don't <u>know</u>. We believe, we think, we hope, we may even trust that we have an inkling of God's "will" for us. It is vanity to use God's name as an authority for our beliefs. To "take the Lord's name in vain" is to say, or even believe, that we know what He/She wants. It has nothing to do with cussing.

Think about it: what does it really mean to "take the Lord's name in vain?" Is it to swear and cuss? Is it to think or claim that we know what God wants?

Love, Grampa

Dear Grandchildren,

I have not written for some time, not that it matters, since the postal service here is bad! It's not like you are getting mail from me on a regular basis! Harry wanted to make a mailbox and put it near shore. His sense of humor gets morbid at times!

It has been raining almost steadily for a week now, and we are getting desperate for sunshine to dry everything and to raise our spirits. Visibility is so poor that, even if a boat came within a mile of us, we wouldn't be able to see it. When I mentioned that to Melanie earlier today, she reminded me of our original pact to look, talk, appear, and <u>be</u> positive.

Which brings me back to an interesting thought I wrote about a little over a week ago: Decisions we make, large or small, stay with us. This is important; it bears repeating, for it helps us to avoid that "I left undone those things which I ought to have done and did those things which I ought not to have done" feeling. Everything we do, or say, or think has consequences. Our past lives in our present. Now, bear with me as I run with this briefly. I know I am repeating myself, but this is especially important for young people, no, for us all!

Choices we make lead to consequences. That's obvious, isn't it? But we must keep firmly in mind that our past never leaves us; we all carry "baggage" from what is supposedly over and done with. Back to basics: choices are important, because they shape our future. So, kids, when you make an unwise choice it lives on in your lives. When you make a good choice, it lives on, also! So? Try to think through each decision that faces you and imagine what it will feel like someday down the road, and also what results it will have for you and those around you. You

may think no one notices. But how do you know? If someone, who perhaps admires you, sees you do something inconsiderate or ill advised, maybe s/he will copy you! Do you really want something you do to diminish or mislead someone else?

I must confess that I carry some guilt feelings with me. I've done a few things that I never should have done, and they haunt me at times. I also have many regrets about "good" things I should have done, but didn't. Will I be more specific than that? No. Sorry.

I will stop here with a fundamental truth: Always be aware of "The Isness of the Was," which I mentioned in an earlier letter.

Choose and act wisely with an eye to future ramifications of what your behavior may reap, even when it comes to "little" choices. And the obvious: be very careful who you choose for friends, what you swallow or inhale, and how you treat your parents.

As I lie here looking up at our Styrofoam ceiling, with all those folded letters stuck in it, I am struck by the futility of all this. I write a letter to you, fold it carefully and stick it in another slot above me. And there they hang, all of them in two neat rows, staring back at me. And I'm thinking that I am just an old fool; who am I kidding, hoping that someday you will have the chance to read them? What are the chances we will be rescued? Or if we are not found, what are the chances that someone will discover our gully shelter, barely visible as it is, even when looking toward it from a hundred yards away? Part of me wants to pull them all down and throw them into the ocean, to be done with it, to accept my fate, correction, <u>our</u> fate. Like Job, of the Old Testament, I want to curse God and shake my fist at Him. But I hesitate, stop to think, and breathe a little prayer for calmness. So, of course, I will not share these thoughts with Melanie or Harry, for we have our little pact to stay positive, optimistic, hopeful. Nor will I destroy all my hard work by casting the letters into the surf. I stopped writing, just lying here looking up. Thinking.

Maybe if someday you do read these letters, this gloomy paragraph will help you to understand things here a little better, to have a sense of our darker moods.

I love you, and I hope this blasted rain stops soon!

Love, Grampa

Dear Grandchildren,

A cold start for the day; we could see our breath and mostly kept our hands pulled up into our sleeves as we went for our walk. It was during that walk that Melanie commented about our food supply. "We've got to stop collecting food from near our shelter," she said. "When winter really sets in, we'll wish we had gathered food from the far ends of the island and saved the nearer foodstuffs for later!"

With that we completely changed our harvesting plans. Now we are suddenly committed to hiking to the far ends of the island for clams, periwinkles, sea lettuce, and the little, 4 to 8 inch long, spiny-backed fish we are able to net from time to time. At both ends of our island we re-arranged rocks around tidal pools, thus creating traps of sorts, in which we are able to occasionally trap larger fish. On one occasion we were able to catch a fast moving octopus that we surprised when we turned over a rock near the low tide mark. We bashed him with a rock to stop him, as we were afraid we might get "bitten" by the hidden beak if we grabbed him with our bare hands. The creature measured something like four feet when we spread it out on a rock after we killed it. We boiled him then chewed, and chewed, and chewed, until we could swallow each bite. I knew calamari was tough, but boiled octopus is just as tough!

Thus we were able to put starvation off a bit. It is our fondest hope that when winter settles in and snow falls, we will be able to find food closer to "home." We shall see.

As we weaken, foraging will become harder. So it is not just the threat of winter weather that motivates us to range farther in our food collecting.

We have learned one important lesson: there are surprising reserves of inner strength waiting to be called upon within each of us. I suggest that you look within yourselves, for I believe that strength is within each of you. Ask God to help you as you try to become adults of strong character, able to withstand adversity, overcome hardship, and prevail just when you doubt you can. There is something more important than mere physical strength, and it is deep within you. Trust that it is there, and even in smaller matters of uncertainty or discouragement, reach inside yourself, and with God's help, find it and use it. That spirit world that I wrote about awhile back is as much a part of you as your hair, or your stomach, or your toenails; you just may not notice it right now.

In the meantime we continue to keep our eyes to seaward whenever the fog is thin enough, or on occasion absent, and we are able to see any significant distance.

Love, Grampa

Dear Grandkids,

Today we held our Island Wide Ecumenical Service sitting in the fog. When we finished reciting the Lord's Prayer, Melanie asked who would be the usher to take the morning offering today. That amused us! Harry brought up his disgust with himself regarding some investments he had made a year ago. That got us to talking about money and personal finances. It also got us to chuckling about how irrelevant that is to our situation here.

"Maybe it's not so irrelevant," I observed. "We certainly have to show very careful stewardship of our meager resources, do we not?" Our conversation wandered off topic to go into detail about what we had and how we might best use everything to give ourselves the best and longest chances of survival.

Now that we are back near our shelter writing letters, I'd like to share some thoughts about money and our stewardship of it. My goal is for you to take a look at the long term before you act in the now. Don't make the mistake so many young people do these days. They want to start out in their adult life where their parents left off when they retired. They want a lovely home, nice car, and all the possessions that accumulate over the years. So they put themselves dangerously deep in debt to have what they want. Don't get suckered into that trap! Live within your means. That means don't buy something you cannot afford. Pay off your credit card completely every month. Be patient and hold off gratification until you can afford it.

Of course, there are some things you must pay for over time: a house, maybe a car, and probably college tuition. In a nutshell, my financial advice to you is simple. Don't get carried away trying to spend more than you should. Be patient. Wait a few years before you take that trip, or buy that larger home, or get a new car. It may be mildly frustrating now, but it will prevent you from being painfully in debt later. "Spend, spend, spend," may be the motto of many of your friends. But it must never be your motto!

Handle each dollar twice while you think about how you will spend it. Gramma Ella and I have done that and we are not sorry. Well, I am a certainly sorry I'm not with her now to enjoy what we <u>do</u> have!

Love, Grampa

Dear Grandkids-Growing-Into-Adults,

One other thing I have mentioned in past letters is the life raft canisters. Harry even made that special dive just to look for them back in August, but to no avail, as you may recall from my earlier letter. "With all the heavy storm surf we have had, maybe the hull has shifted," Harry insisted.

Harry has been insisting for several days now that he should make another try, only this time more to the west of here, since the currents sometimes seem to drift that way. Melanie and I strongly argue against it. She even went so far as to threaten that if he did make such a dive, in this colder weather and colder water, she would not have anything to do with it; he would be entirely on his own. Her point? It is now far too risky and we are not as strong as we were back then. For him to make the dive now would probably be fatal. I agreed. So far we have dissuaded Harry from making the attempt. But as our situation grows more desperate, and our health continues to decline, we are torn between facing the future together, come what may, or taking the chance that we might retrieve one of the canisters, even if there would probably be only two of us to use it.

The blow to our morale that Harry's death would cause is unthinkable. The saying "two's company; three's a crowd," does not apply when you are three people stranded on an uninhabited island facing winter, and eventually, death. There is no way I can convey to you how crucial a third person is to our psychological well being. Would that we were four, or more!

Back to the canister. On the other hand, and there is always an "on the other hand" consideration. With winter closing in, our situation is becoming more desperate. Maybe we should take the chance and have Harry make a short dive or two, spaced several days apart. We know where some large parts of our vessel lie to the southwest of our shelter, just beyond the rocks. Maybe, just maybe, we might find a canister, but, no, that is highly unlikely after these months.

Harry insisted. We resisted. He began the day by announcing, "I want that other canister from the boat. I am going to dive for it today. The water is calm and the swell is minimal. It's now or never."

We argued until we were blue in the face, but to no avail.

Right after lunch we prepared. Harry donned as much clothing as he could get into, slipped Fred's oversized rain gear over everything, and into the ice water he went.

He came up from the first dive with a huge grin on his face. "I think I can get it!" And he did. It took him two more dives before the canister bobbed to the surface, bent and scratched, but floating! We waded out as he pushed it toward us. We hauled it up above the high tide mark and went to work stripping Harry, wrapping him in blankets and the smelly sealskin, and pressing our warm bodies against him. "I'm too old for this crap!" he muttered through blue lips and chattering teeth. Eventually his shivering stopped, his blue lips regained their normal pink color, and he was able to make sense when he talked.

After a meal of hot seaweed, periwinkles, and boiled grain soup, we opened the canister.

As we hoped, it contained a life raft. But when we pulled the pin to inflate it with its compressed air bottle, we discovered several large tears in the flotation sacks. So our hopes of having a seaworthy craft ended. But, we had already agreed, where would we go with it? The good news is that it will prove an excellent "ground cover" inside our gully shelter, to provide a moisture barrier between us and the rocky floor with its trickling brook beneath it. So that's our task for tomorrow: to install it. Then there is the stash of energy bars, biscuits in tins, and trail mix. We found vitamin tablets, ten jugs of drinking water, ten of those thin, bright orange highly insulated, thermal blankets, three flashlights, a compass, and fishing line with fishhooks.

One more BIG step toward lengthening our survival time!

I'm tired, so will end this for now. Never give up hope, kids, never. It is darkest before the dawn. You have something you need to accomplish, a long term paper, rebuilding a friendship, saving money for a car or college? Persevere! Stick to it! You may be surprised at the results.

Love, Grampa

Dear Grandchildren,

A chilly day greeted us when we crawled out of our shelter this morning: no fog, but a hazy atmosphere that limited visibility to a mile or so. We guess the temperature was around 45° to 50° when we ate breakfast. As the day wore on, the haze thickened and the air felt more and more damp. Our walk warmed us up for a while. But by mid afternoon we were chilly and had to add a layer of clothes.

We dragged the flattened life raft into our shelter this morning, and smoothed it out as best we could. It will make a wonderful ground cover, insulating us against the moisture rising from the water running under our damp stone floor. The sail has helped, but it gradually had become soaked by the moisture rising from the little creek running under the stone floor. The raft is large enough that we were able to use sticks to prop the edges up on each side against the rock walls, thus providing a moisture barrier of sorts.

Our conversation, as we sat at the top of the island near Spinnaker Rock turned to our relationships together. Although we sometimes feel irritated at each other; who wouldn't, what with being confined these ninety-one days with only two companions apiece, we get along well, out of necessity, I guess.

I said something about "love your neighbor as yourself." Melanie picked up on it and suggested that we have to love ourselves to be able to love others. That led into a two hour chat about how to go about that: how to accept our faults and weaknesses, how to embrace who and what we are, without getting caught up in pride or shame. After all this time we thought we knew each other well, but the revelations, good and bad, that we shared today were most interesting, and it brought us even closer together. It was a delightful afternoon: one that each of us will cherish for a long time.

So now, my grandchildren, let me pass on some more grandfatherly advice. I remember that, when I was a teenager, I often felt inadequate and sometimes found myself disliking who I was: my complexion, my body, my shyness, my lack of wisdom, my impulsive and foolish acts. I'm sure you know what I am talking about. I would argue with my parents about something and feel spent, ashamed, and powerless when it was all over. After all, they were the bosses and I was, more often than not, wrong in what I was arguing. At those times, loving myself was virtually impossible!

But deeper than that is something else. You are a child of God, created, in some manner, in His image. Let that sink in for a while, and then look inside to discover and lay hold of that worthiness, that loveliness, that enduring self that resides within you. Love yourself and as you do so, over the years, you will discover that it frees you to be more loving and accepting of others.

The world is a better place for our being able to do so. Yada, yada, yada. Forgive me if I sound "preachy." Well, I am a chaplain, after all, so what did you expect? Think about this. That's all I ask: think about it, and pray about it, or should I say meditate deeply about it. If I ever see you again, I hope I will discover that each of you has a healthy, vibrant self-love.

Love, Grampa

Dear Grandkids,

Today was a low morale day. In addition to the gloomy fog and the howling gale force winds, we considered our future, not a happy thing.

It began when we were sitting up near spinnaker rock, staring into the misty fog. Harry asked, half to himself and half to us, "Will we survive?"

Melanie replied sharply, "Harry! You know the rule. We ought not to bring this up for discussion."

"Look at us, Mel!" he replied. "Skin and bones. We look like survivors of a World War II POW camp!" He was right.

So we talked. We talked about the colder weather that we are feeling, the relentless fog, the constant high winds, how much harder it is to rouse ourselves to go for our long walks, the evermore difficult search for food, the obvious nutritional needs we were not meeting (even with the vitamins), and so on. And, of course we talked about the very few days when visibility was good enough to even see a boat if there was one out there.

The weather is slowly worsening, and our health is slowly declining. What to do? One thing we have done is limit ourselves to one daily walk, making sure we go to the farthest ends of the island to scrounge for whatever edibles we can gather. By now there isn't much forage available near our shelter. We are tired and we need what energy we have to feed ourselves and accomplish the daily chores of our survival.

As we sat together beside the brightly colored spinnaker, a terrible silence fell over us. I felt myself on the verge of tears. Melanie saved the day by muttering, "Dear God, we're running out of hope. Please help us to find strength." Her voice drifted off.

In response, after a few moments of quiet, Harry spoke, also very softly, "We need to know that you are near us, God."

And I added, "We know your Spirit is always near, always within us, ever present."

Our words seemed futile, self-conscious attempts at an optimism we did not feel.

But then a strange thing happened. Melanie, to her own surprise as well as ours, as Melanie confessed later, began to sing Amazing Grace. We joined in. That was followed by "Abide with Me," mournfully singing the next phrase, "the darkness deepens," and faithfully singing the ending, "Lord with me abide. When other helpers fail and comforts flee, help of the helpless, oh, abide with me!" Then we sang, "Spirit of God, Descend Upon My Heart." Tears of joy trickled down our cheeks. Can you believe that could have happened? Does this make any sense to you as you read this? How could we feel joyful at this juncture in our lives? Some moments later, with no conscious intentions on our parts, we stood, our hands reached out and we leaned together as our psyches and spirits linked! I cannot explain to you how this epiphany came about. But I feel compelled to write of it.

For some strange reason, which I cannot find words to express, everything was suddenly okay. Our future together, hopeless or not, shrank into insignificance! We were no longer trapped on a dismal island, darkened by heavy fog and pessimism. It was as if we were on a mountaintop, sunshine and view almost taking our breath away, one of those "mountaintop experiences" that mystics and spiritual people tell us about. And it was happening to us.

I don't know if we'll ever be the same again after this.

Love, Grampa

Dear Grandkids,

We got a big scare today! After breakfast, when were walking up toward the mid island depression, the earth started to shake! There was a deep rumbling sound. You could feel it in your chest. And the whole island seemed to be shaking! I had to use a boulder nearby to keep from falling. Harry and Melanie had presence of mind enough to sit right down where they were. Or maybe, as Harry said later, they fell down and it just <u>looked</u> like they knew what they were doing!

After what seemed like minutes, though it was probably less than a minute, the shaking subsided, leaving us mentally shaken. I said, "Holy shit!" See how I, the religious leader, used the word "holy" to add dignity to my pronouncement.

Melanie said, "Wow! Wow! Wow!"

Harry asked, "What the hell was that?"

I remember our exact words, as that was a most memorable moment for us!

We concluded that it must have been an earthquake. You most likely have already figured that out. Melanie suggested that maybe the storm had deposited us on an island somewhere along the Pacific "rim of fire" that makes up much of California, Alaska, the Aleutian Islands, and Japan. Of course we could only speculate, as we had no idea where that long ago storm pushed us. Has it been more than one hundred days already?

We were left with a disquieting thought: What if Melanie was correct and what if an eruption was coming? We tossed that around for a while and decided that such an event was highly unlikely. Not that we could do anything about it. To which I cocked an eyebrow, grinned a lopsided smirk, looked skyward and commented, "I hope you're listening, God!"

At that instant our island was hit with a brief aftershock. Melanie, bless her soul, suggested that I should have been more respectful when I talked to God. And we laughed, which turned into a fit of nervous giggles for a few minutes. Harry added, "Well at least it wasn't a lightning bolt from Heaven!"

So that was our excitement for the day.

Love, Grampa

Good evening to you!

It has been windy and around freezing all day. The fog has been thin; we can see our entire island and some of the ocean surface.

As you already know, Melanie has been experimenting all along with plants and roots. Today she discovered a plant with a parsnip-like flavor! Harry was today's guinea pig, so he ate some of it. We waited for any ill effects, and there were none. So we harvested a few fists full of them and brought them back to our gully where we split them open and retrieved the innards. We will boil them tomorrow and have a feast, that is if Harry has not developed any "discomforts" by then.

We huddled in the lee of our firepit and went over Melanie's copious notes and drawings of sea and land plants we have tested. There are many pages of drawings and observations about taste, aftereffects, and different ways we have prepared them. Might be an interesting document to share with the world when/if we get out of here. Although one wonders who would really care about survival foods on this cold, rocky, scrap of land in the middle of nowhere.

Did I mention the mountain? I may have, but I don't really want to go back and read the dozens of letters I've folded and stashed in the Styrofoam ceiling. Well, it's true, we have a mountain, but it is way off in the distance across a rough and wide stretch of water. We spotted it way back in July, or thereabouts, and have often wondered if it was another island and if it had any people on it. We speculate that maybe the occasional boat specks we have seen off in the distance might have come from there. That would be good news and tends to magnify our halfhearted hopes of eventual rescue.

Hope is a word with many shades of meaning. Hope includes faith, trust, and belief. As I recall somewhere it was written that "faith is the assurance of things hoped for the conviction of things not seen." Give that some thought, will you? This doesn't just apply to wanting to escape a bad situation. It also applies to living faithfully, anticipation that the world of the spirit is real, and that we are and will always be a part of it, a sense of confidence that good will triumph over evil.

A question that we all ask at times: Why do bad things happen to good people? Or, for that matter, why do good things happen to bad people? There is evil in our world, and we are distressed by it. But, is "evil" actually bad? I mean, what if only good things happened to good people and what if bad people had only bad things happen to them? Where would the need for faith come in? You'd think bad people would start being good, and that good people would keep on living as good people. Why would anyone need to pray, to ask God for help and guidance? Then there's this: God gave us free will, and some of us make bad choices based on our bad experiences, such as illness, natural disaster, or mean things done to us by others. So?

Does that not impel us into thinking about good and evil? And, if so, does that not lead to a desire for goodness, kindness, charity, and love? Are our strivings for faith and our attempts at being good people partly a result of the "bad" we have seen? We cannot know "God's Plan." In his infinite wisdom, which we cannot begin to comprehend, has He created a world in which faith, rather than absolutely certain knowing, is a fundamental part of who we are as human beings? I think it is a good thing that "now we see through a glass darkly, then face to face." If God granted us certainty about Eternal futures wouldn't we be mere puppets worked by God's "hand?"

And, I have trouble dealing with the view that everything that happens to a person is God's plan, that being spared in a disaster or killed by a lightning bolt is God at work, manipulating every facet of our physical world. I've watched the news on TV when a survivor of a train wreck or plane crash thanks God that he was spared. Is not the corollary to that that God killed or maimed those who were less fortunate in that event? Can a person with Parkinson's Disease, or lung cancer, or some other debilitating condition be happy that God did this to him? If I live a healthy life, can I simply say, "thank you God" and assume that He did this for me? No way! We live in a world of chance; we grow in a world of faith. We ask God for inward help and guidance, for strength and patience, for compassion and love, for self-understanding and charitable views of others. God is spirit and we are, in part, also spirit. What happens in the physical world, good or bad, is perhaps designed to shake our souls so that we look around, spiritually, for meanings and realities that last. Eternity makes today's fortunes significant not for their happening, but for what we may learn from them, for the focus beyond what we see and hear and feel happening. I like the suggestions that some science fiction writers offer: images of "another world" of a "parallel universe" of something beyond what we sense in our daily lives. In their novels they tap us on the shoulder and ask us to look beyond the here and now.

When I weep with sadness at horrible and painful things that occur in the world, I am compelled by LOVE, to reach out, at least in spirit, to the "victims" of such things. And what if the "victim" is me? Then I reach inward to God, and to my faith that I am always and everywhere in His care. This does not make me happy with bad things that happen; but it does lead me to a fork in my inner road; one leads to despair, the other to faith. My free will, which has its limits, of course, including the ability to conceive of Greater Realities, makes it possible for the "Image of God" within me to "Become." I have long ago concluded that the "image of God" within me, is a spiritual fact of life. I can try to be in touch with that "God-self" within or I can turn my focus to the physical world and gradually lose my sense of the spiritual.

We should all go one step further with this spirit world notion. I am convinced that the world of the spirit is an interconnected world; that you and I and part of the same invisible network. When a group prays for a person in difficulty, there is an invisible link that can provide some strength and guidance and hope. There is no proof for this. But I know it is true.

I hope all this has confused you. I pray that you are perplexed enough about all this to make a fresh start at seeking deep spiritual understandings, understandings as deep as your human limitations will allow. And I like to think that the ongoing results of a fresh start will pull you and push you toward the kind of spiritual awakening that will comfort and strengthen you in spirit.

Oops. It's so dark I can't read what I have just scribbled. That's it for this short day!

Love, Grampa

Dear Grandkids,

We have been in the grip of icy rain, and sometimes freezing fog, for a week now. Today it is cold, cold, cold! We wrap cloth around our faces, and our breath freezes into a white border around the cloth where our mouths are. I have never experienced fog that freezes, although I have seen pictures of it at places like the weather station at the top of Mt. Washington in New Hampshire. There must be an inch or more of this hoarfrost. I think that's what they call it. It coats anything that sticks up into the moving air. I can tell you we were most appreciative of the thermal blankets piled on us during the night. Those, along with the smelly seal skins, fur side against our bodies, kept us toasty warm.

One good thing about all this, I guess: The gulls have been hunkered down and are a bit slow on the uptake when we approach them with our net. We have tied small stones to the edges of the net, weighing it in such a way that, when it is thrown it circles, drops, and traps the gulls. So we have some fresh meat!

We know the sun is "up there" somewhere, but you can't prove it by us!

In reference to my October 12th letter about evil. I don't think anyone has an answer to explain the problem of good and evil. I simply believe that, although there are some things that are simply "unknowable," good and evil exist. Where it comes from or what to do about it is never easy. For me, I have to believe that God is some kind of benevolent, "clockmaker" who has set "the whole thing" in motion. To some religious people that is a heresy. They want to believe that God micromanages his Creation and that everything is all "part of His plan." "Not a sparrow falls…." By the way, that bit about "not a sparrow falls," does not say that God prevents the sparrow from falling, only that He cares. Kind of makes a point, don't you think? I can't find it within me to love a God who directly causes suffering. For me I must see God as spirit and the universe and free will as simply "the way it is."

The key to understanding, if understanding is at all possible, has to be to look to the spirit world within us, and to find there some sort of personal faith that when our bodies die our place in the spirit world continues. To me that translates into the simple affirmation that God is with me always.

It works for me, most of the time! Despite this terrible fix Melanie, Harry and I find ourselves in, I find comfort in being in God's hands. I hope that this works for all of you, someday, if not yet.

Love, Grampa

Dear Grandkids,

The sun broke through today! That may seem trivial to you, so let me explain.

We have been trapped in a long spell of rain and fog. Day after day, we awoke to the patter of rain, and sometimes sleet, on our sailcloth roof, the sound of wind against our shelter, and the roar of surf. We bundled up to go out each day, foraged in the rain for some greenery to eat, and finished the last of our smoked fish on Tuesday and our seal meat yesterday. Oh yes, we have killed and cooked three seals since September 6th, and it has not gotten any easier!

Fishing improved in August when we discovered several rock formations along the shore that each had but one opening for fish to enter and leave. It was a fairly simple matter to hang the net at the opening and then splash around in the water to drive any fish toward the ocean. Not as effective as it sounds, as usually the "pockets" were empty or the fish managed to streak past the net, leaving us frustrated and the proud owners of an empty net!!

We spread everything we own on rocks around our little palace, anchoring them down with stones. It looked like a tornado had trashed a whole neighborhood and strewn belongings everywhere! Although it was chilly and breezy, we managed to find individual spots behind rock formations where we could lie in the sun in our underwear and soak up the welcome rays. The gusts were chilly on the skin, but our discomfort was more than offset by the pleasure of drying out and feeling that weak warmth of the sun.

This afternoon we strolled along the higher parts of our island and reveled in the brilliant sparkle of the sun on the ruffled ocean water. The wind and brightness made my eyes water, but the boost that all this brilliance and beauty gave to our spirits was most welcome. The distant mountain, white with a cloak of snow, caught and held our attention. Naturally, we strained our eyes searching for a boat out there somewhere, but to no avail.

No mini sermon today, kids. Well, maybe a small one: <u>Appreciate beauty</u>! While feeling hugely satisfied by Mother Nature's display of sun and surf, I would give anything to be able to see tall trees or to browse through an art gallery, or even a shopping mall, or even my living room, come to think of it! Oh, how we miss what we used to take for granted! When life gives you a lemon, admire its lovely yellow skin.

Harry suggested that sun on snow would be beautiful to see, to which Melanie and I pointed to the snow draped mountain, and responded with thumbs down and loud boos. We await the coming winter with dread. And we hope the seals will continue to clamber up on shore. Soon we will have to eat some of our precious canned goods.

Love, Grampa

Dear Grandchildren,

We are really pleased with our sail covered home in the gully! In fact, in the miserable fog this morning we all walked around it smiling like fools. "You look happy," Melanie commented to me. I nodded and agreed that I not only looked happy, but that I was happy! How could that be, we wondered. Here we are marooned on a miserable, cold island with little hope of rescue, and we're happy???

What is happiness, anyway? We chatted about that for a while and concluded that happiness is not a goal in life. It is a byproduct. We have all known people who struggled and strived to be happy, but ended up unhappy. As an aside, let me make this comment: Money does not buy happiness. There are sad and troubled rich people, just as there are happy and fulfilled poor people. The same kind of thing can be said of fame or good looks or power. Happiness, or unhappiness for that matter, is a result that emerges from how we live our lives, from the values and good motives that have guided us.

So, the way I see it, kids, is this: Live your life so that you can be satisfied you have done the best you could with it. As the scouts put it, be "trustworthy, loyal, helpful, friendly, courteous, kind, obedient, cheerful, thrifty, brave, clean and reverent," and the byproduct will be a sense of fulfillment, contentment, and satisfaction that you'd done your best. If that ain't happiness, what is? Not only can you not buy happiness, but you can't usually obtain it by striving for it. Innumerable people have found that just when happiness is in their grasp, it slips away. On the other hand, I have known dozens of people who dealt with chronic illness, personal loss, and the approach of death with an inner sense of peace, which I would label happiness.

Love your neighbor as you also love yourself. Love God and trust that somehow you are in "His" presence. Happiness will emerge. Don't try to find it; let it find you!

Now permit me to shed a sad tear or two, here in the midst of my happiness, as I say goodnight, missing all of you with all my heart!

Love, Grampa

Dear Loved Ones,

This will be a short note to tell you about the weather.

Today was bitter cold. There is no doubt that the temperature was far below freezing, as the puddles froze solid, except the deepest ones. We could break through the ice by stomping on it. The wind chill factor must be in the teens! This is by far the coldest day yet.

I dare to hope that the weather will not stay this cold, as the weather generally has been above freezing this month.

As you may have concluded, Melanie Pickett, Harry O'Toole, and I have had hundreds of hours in which to talk together and share our thoughts, feelings, and personal histories. We have learned incredible amounts of information about virtually everything in each other's past lives. We know things about each other that we would never have even imagined had our relationships not been confined to this place. What a privilege to know so much about another person! And how often we have commented that it is too bad people do not have such an opportunity to share themselves. We are immeasurably enriched by our knowledge of each other.

I believe that sharing myself with others helps to make the world a better place. Too many people are so self-contained that they do not allow others to see who they really are. They put up a front, to protect themselves, and in the bargain lose the opportunity for meaningful intimacy with another person.

When you think about it, what is the value of hiding your inner motivations, thoughts, hopes, and fears? Of course personal secrecy protects you against the negative judgments of others who are unable to accept you as you really are deep down inside. Maybe that's important for you. But I would rather lose a so-called friend because he or she didn't like what they saw when I revealed my true self to them. Who needs superficial friends? On the other hand, there are secrets from our past that are best left unshared. We do not want to hurt someone by revealing things we have done that we ought not to have done.

Yes, sharing of our selfhood with others is sometimes difficult and sometimes unwise. But the benefits of being known and knowing are huge. My better friends are people with whom I have shared myself and who have reciprocally shared themselves with me. So here's my advice to you. Be open with others, and invite them to be open with you. Trust others to honor your secrets. You will be hurt and offended when someone betrays your trust by sharing things you intended to be private exchanges with a friend. But the other side of that coin is a deepened sense of love and understanding of those around you with whom you have shared your inner self and your personal history. How else can we interpret the Biblical injunction to love your neighbor as yourself? Dare to share! But understand the risks.

Love, Grampa

Dear Grandkids,

Today Harry remarked about our different religious backgrounds, how compatible we were with each other's faith, and how insignificant were our religious differences. As you may recall, he was raised in a Roman Catholic family, and Melanie's family was Jewish. That led to a discussion about how we treat people of different faiths. We agreed that it is not possible, nor logical to believe one religious group knows the true answers.

Our discussion led me to start thinking about all those fundamentalist religious groups who claim their sacred writings, and their creeds are right and the rest are wrong. My idea of God does not allow room for exclusiveness that claims one creed is right and the others are wrong. So how should we deal with someone whose beliefs are different from ours?

I can reason with that person and try to persuade them that they are wrong. But what does that accomplish? If I can't convince him (or her), we are left farther apart than before I tried to do so. If I can convince him, am I guilty of "pulling the rug out from under him?" Have I taken away something of personal value without replacing it with something of equal or greater value?

Fundamentalists have found a comforting and meaningful way of dealing with death and what is beyond. If they believe their faith, their savior, or their sacred book guarantees them eternal life, what right do I have to try to change that? And why should I? For many such believers the simple answers they have found gives them comfort and strength to deal with end of life issues in a hopeful and satisfying way. As I wrote a while back, agnostics and atheists scoff at such religion as a crutch. Maybe they are right to scoff. But maybe that's what religion is for many people. Is that a bad thing? Is it bad to face death with a sense of trust in the goodness and power of their god?

It only offends me when some religious "fanatics," tell me I am headed to Hell or oblivion if I don't believe as they do. Whenever I hear someone use language to put down a person whose faith is different, it hurts my sensibilities and it angers me.

Demeaning others because they believe differently, is wrong, inconsiderate, mean-spirited and unfair. It also demonstrates a religious view that makes God less than an all loving, spirit. Would God, who is Love, really "save" a chosen few and discard all the other good (and bad) people in the world, just because they did not affirm one particular creed? Believing God would do so would make the world a place that mocks the idea of a loving God.

Any religion, whether group or individual that asserts that it has the One and Only Truth and rejects all other claims, in effect, denies that God loves all mankind. I cannot believe in, worship, nor want to be associated with such a small, separatist god.

So I will be friends with those who think I am going to Hell or into oblivion when my body dies. I will agree to disagree with them. There is little point in arguing with people whose minds are made up. Nor do I wish to shake their faith, for it gives them comfort and strength to face life with all its difficulties.

But in my heart of hearts I will say, "We are all in God's care and keeping." And that is good enough for me, and with that belief I rest my case and affirm my trust in God.

Love God, trust God, and don't let anyone convince you that there is only one way to salvation and life eternal.

Love, Grampa

To all of my loved ones,

Last night we had a serious ice storm! We had to pound on our Styrofoam and driftwood framed door to get it to open! We were greeted by a horrible and beautiful sight: sun sparkling on a brilliant coating of ice.

Thankfully, the sun warmed the island enough to melt most of it during the day, and the wind died off to a mere 10 to 15 miles per hour. That's like a dead calm around here!

We found a two foot long fish swimming around in one of the pool traps we made at the east end of the island. "He died to make us well," Harry commented as we cleaned it. This led to another round of talk about salvation, eternity, and life after death, while we waited for our fish to cook. The fish made a satisfying feast once we hauled his carcass out of the coals we had put him in earlier that afternoon. Melanie sliced the cooked fish into strips and fried them in seal blubber to make the meal a bit tastier and to provide us with some fat.

We batted the idea of "forever" around for a while and then settled in to write our after dinner letters, before it got too dark to see what we were writing. This leads me to -----

"Are you saved?" the Devout Christian asks. A "yes" brings a warm smile of Christian Fellowship. And "I'm not sure" brings a flood of assurance that if only you will "Accept Jesus as your personal Lord and Savior" you will, in fact, be saved. A "no" response brings a frown of concern and a shake of the head.

What is "salvation?" It means, put simply, that God has saved your soul from damnation, hell, or oblivion. It means that Eternal Life has been granted to you. It is a great cause for celebration among believers, worry among agnostics and concern among thinkers.

Eternity and infinity are concepts that are well beyond the ability of the human mind to imagine. There is an old Chinese proverb, concerning the limits of the human mind; it goes something like this: "Try to imagine a perfectly straight endless hole from where you are off into space." You will soon imagine an end. There has to be one. Then you will wonder what's beyond the end. There has to be more. So the hole continues in your imagination. Ending and not ending. You cannot imagine either possibility: neither an end nor endlessness. One finds in this proverb a bit of advice for all "believers" in eternal life. Namely this: our human understanding is limited.

Think about the many opinions expressed by "believers." A Native American of our earlier American days looked forward, when he died, to living a life of endless warfare and buffalo hunting. A Moslem fanatic assumes that when he blows himself up he will go to a heaven where he will be served and serviced forever by a group of comely young virgins. Usually the virgins' thoughts on this matter are ignored, of course. One wonders what those comely young maidens concept of eternal life is like! A Christian imagines sitting on a cloud with a harp, or living in a mansion in Heaven. Another imagines being absorbed into the great spiritual stream of eternity. My point? There are many wildly divergent views of what awaits us in the next life. None of them are more than speculation, or hope, or faith, or belief. As I commented earlier, "now we see through a glass darkly; then face to face."

Because we are human, our minds cannot truly comprehend eternity (endless time), infinity (endless space) or salvation (endless life beyond the grave). So let's end the silly and flagrant self-righteousness that claims our view of salvation is the one and only true view! And that the other views are so much silly speculation. Let's have faith that God, or Allah, or Yahweh forever takes care of us. Once we have that faith let us affirm the ancient eastern philosopher's view that "All roads of religion ascend the mountain of the Lord and meet at the top."

Salvation is our great hope and our great unknown. So? Live with not knowing. Do the best you can with the life you have been given. After all my years of studying theology I can summarize my entire personal theology in seven words: "I am in God's care and keeping."

Likewise I believe that the same is true for you!

That's it for today. Despite everything (the worsening weather, our dwindling food supply, our growing concern that we will never be rescued, and all the other negative aspects of our situation) our spirits have been up of late. Don't ask me why!

Love, Grampa

Dear Grandkids,

Two things:

One: we had a blizzard today, but most of the snow blew away in the howling gale force winds. Our gully filled with snow and we spent several hours cleaning it out by pushing and pulling it into wind suit jackets and then flicking the jackets in the wind, where the snow was instantly transported somewhere miles to the east.

Two: I may have mentioned our growing wood pile? We have scrounged every piece of wood we can find anywhere on our shores and stacked it in any depression that promises to protect it from being blown away. Yes, the winds are sometimes strong enough to grab driftwood and flip it end over end, or roll it for some distance. We think we have enough wood to keep the fire burning for a couple of months. We try to "keep a stiff upper lip, old chap," as Melanie often puts it, even as we feel the coming winter's ominous advance upon us. Sometime in January or February we will be out of wood. That will mean no fire: no cooking, no warmth.

However, there is some cause for hope. I don't think I have written about it, but we have harvested eight chunks of tundra/peat, or whatever its real name is, from the bog in the depression behind our shelter. It was incredibly hard work using our serrated knife and our hatchet. After a difficult struggle to free them from their surroundings, we took the foot-square chunks and stacked them along the inside walls of our firepit to dry. It seems to be working. They are getting quite dry feeling. So in another day or so we may try using them for fuel.

We are jealous of you when you are out playing in the snow, or shoveling it, or putting a piece of wood on the fire in your fireplace. But not very! Well, maybe about the fire in the fireplace.

And now a word from your grandfather, the chaplain. In my view, there are two important forces in our world:

One is the need to be rescued. We have a need to be rescued, from pain, loneliness, crime, illness, injury, poverty, disability, boredom, uncertainty, death, and the list goes on. The need to be rescued often becomes a need for power and control over the world around us, which may lead to all manner of unfortunate twists and turns in our inner life and in our outer behavior. But this need also results in motives and behaviors that make the world a better place when good folks try to rescue others from their problems.

The second is the need for love. We have a need for affection, respect, kindness, friendship, companionship, and this list also goes on. It gets perverted when in the quest for love, individuals look for it in the wrong places, and seek it by counterproductive behavior. On the other hand, for many good men and women, there is a need to love others and to try to be rescuers. Many organizations expend great amounts of time, talent, and energy to prove love and rescue. Such groups, and also individuals, also make our world a better place.

Love, Grampa

Dear Grandchildren,

The "peat globs" as Harry calls them burn poorly, but they do burn! We will harvest more, now that we know they work. Though smoky and slow burning they will be better than nothing! And they radiate precious heat.

I have been thinking about "The Miracle of the Loaves and Fishes" of late. I'd like to share my view of that Bible story with you. Believe me, I have sound reasons for doing so, as the "miracle" of rescue has been constantly on my mind of late.

You will no doubt recall the basics of the story: A huge crowd gathers on a rural hillside to hear Jesus. As the story is interpreted by some, God manufactured food out of thin air to feed the thousands. Not only did God do that, but the disciples "policed" the area afterwards and retrieved baskets of leftover loaves and fishes! A miracle! Or so we are told. But the Bible does not say food was created on the spot.

I have another slant on the story. But first let me say that I do not know the will of God, nor what God can or cannot do. I assume God can do anything. After all he is God!

Suppose this is what actually happened: A huge crowd of people walked for hours out into the wilderness to see and hear this man, Jesus, whose fame was spreading far and wide. Now, let's stop right at this point and ask a practical question: would they have arrived empty-handed? I have several chaplain friends, rabbis, who scoff at that idea! "We are hard headed, practical people, always have been, always will be," one of them once told me. Before a Hebrew of two thousand years ago headed out into a wilderness, he would most assuredly have tucked some dried fish, or a loaf of bread, or a small wineskin into his or her robe. Like those folks today who carry a plastic water bottle and a snack bar with them when they leave the house.

So keep that in mind that as the crowd gathers, most of them have their "snack" tucked away in the pockets of their robes. They listen, enthralled, as Jesus speaks to the multitude. They are profoundly touched by his warmth, his compassion, his spirituality. Their hearts are filled with wonder and love and compassion for those around them. For the moment, at least, they are transformed by a glowing sense of love.

After several hours, Jesus stops talking and a natural intermission occurs. Hungry and thirsty, those who brought food and drink remove the items from their robes and eat, sharing with families and friends who came with them. They notice individuals and groups nearby who have brought nothing with them. Ordinarily they might have said, "Let them go hungry. Maybe next time they'll have sense enough to bring something." But this is no ordinary event, for the charismatic Jesus has touched something deep inside each listener, and as a result of that touching they smile and offer food and drink to those who have none. A warm sense of family pervades the crowd.

After a while Jesus resumes speaking and those who are left with a scrap of bread, or a piece of fish, quietly let it drop to the ground as they are drawn into the mesmerizing words of Jesus. They are no longer hungry or thirsty; they are physically content. Later, when Jesus has finished speaking, the crowd disperses, heading home with a renewed inner sense of love and compassion for their fellow human beings, a warm feeling that something momentous has happened within their souls.

The disciples clean up the leftovers, putting the fish and bread into baskets.

What has happened here? The answer is clear: an <u>inner miracle of the spirit</u> has bonded a huge crowd together in such a way that they willingly and lovingly share what they have with those who have nothing to eat. And to my way of thinking that inner miracle is far more exciting and important than the idea that God did some kind of "manufacturing from thin air" miracle. The miracle of love, now that's exciting, and important, and productive in the field of human relations.

So, dear grandchildren, take this to heart: Love and matters of our inner spirits are far more important in the long run than anything else. For what is seen is passing, but what is unseen is Eternal. And that's important. Don't get psychologically trapped looking for physical miracles when the inward miracle of loving compassion is of far greater significance. May that be as important in your lives as it is in mine!

Love, Grampa

DAY 145
MONDAY, NOVEMBER 20TH, 2006

Dear Grandchildren,

Well, here it is, late in November, and we are experiencing the dreaded change in weather that the season brings! The days are much shorter, and the longer, colder nights eat away at our morale and normally high spirits. This morning was cold! No skim of ice on puddles, and no frost, but cold nevertheless. The sharply cold breeze coming off the water made it feel like it was below freezing, but we guess the temperature was right around 32°. That's the good news!

Now the bad news: late in the morning the snow flurries began. The flakes melted almost as soon as they hit the ground. With the light snow blowing at an angle, we tromped around the island, squinting into the wind from time to time, watching for any boat that might be out in this weather, but not with any real expectation of seeing one.

By the time we reached the seal colony we were unpleasantly surprised to see the area empty of animals. The seals were gone! And with them a major source of food. Maybe they will return after the snow stops falling.

We counted perhaps a hundred seagulls, but they have long since stopped laying eggs. We gave up on eggs as a food source two months ago. Most of the gulls were standing motionless, with their beaks to the wind, while others were soaring about, then landing and appearing to settle in. Netting them will be much harder without their dive bombing of us to protect their eggs.

A heavy squall of thickly falling snow enveloped us as we were heading for lunch in our shelter. We had trouble seeing much more than twenty feet ahead of us. But by now we know this side of the island by heart and had no trouble finding our way home. Interesting that we find our rude shelter in a rocky gully on an uninhabited island to be our home. I am happy to report that the mini blizzard ended almost as quickly as it started.

After a "gourmet meal" of cold, precooked periwinkles and clams, we strolled over to the west end of the island, then up to our chapel rock. We sat up there, squinting through the falling snow, too tired to hike back to our shelter without some rest first. We need to conserve our energy. So, we sat and talked before struggling to our feet and heading back home. We discovered small drifts of snow in the protected leeward sides of rocks and shrubs. By the time we finished with our discussion, and walk, the flurries were over, sun was peaking through breaks in the clouds, and the miniature snow piles were melting.

Now that winter seems to be truly on its way here, we have opted to spend the remainder of the afternoon making a thorough inspection of our shelter, and arranging a large woodpile near the three-sided firepit, in case we get serious snow and find ourselves snowed in and restricted in our movements away from the shelter. We added more stones to the edges of the sail that covers our shelter and the firepit in front of it. Several times, edges of the sail have been torn loose by high winds. Once one entire side of the sail was waving and beating thunderously in a high wind. We had a real struggle to spread it back over the firepit and anchor it with more stones than before. The last thing we want to have happen is for the sail to blow free, rip apart, and be stripped from our little palace during a blizzard!

For supper we boiled some water over the fire, which we now keep banked and alive 24/7, and enjoyed a hot seaweed stew, with wild rose "apples" and some little nut like seeds we have stripped from a tiny shrub that grows near the north end of the island. We had barely enough time to clean the utensils, and write our letters before sunset. The sun sets earlier now.

Wish there was a post office so I could pop this letter in the mail to you. Oh, well, dreams are good to have!

Love, Grampa

Dear Grandkids,

Well, it happened again. Today the puddles froze solid for the first time in almost a week. We have long since brought our bottles of water inside at night, as we don't want to take the chance that they will freeze solid and split the containers. We only have eight bottles to hold liquids, as two of them were damaged, one when a rock fell on it, and one when we left it too near the fire, and it partially melted and collapsed. Two of them blew away during high winds and we never found them.

If the cold lasts, it will at least help to preserve our smoked jerky seal meat strips for a little longer: Mother Nature's refrigerator!

Next time you feel like complaining to your parents, or significant others, about the meal you are served, think of us! We would be happy to share a veggie burger with you, or a fast food hamburger, or even a stale donut! In other words: appreciate what you have. It is no small task to survey everything around you and feel good about it, being thankful it is there, and smiling within because it is there!

We wonder if we will die of malnutrition or hunger during the months ahead. Seagulls are harder to catch now that they are no longer nesting. Seals come and go. Fishing is sporadic at best; and the plants we rely on for food seem to be shutting down for winter. We know that before long snow will cover everything.

Although we have a fairly large cache of canned and packaged foods, the supply is not limitless, and we doubt that there is enough, even if we ration ourselves severely, to get us through the winter that we know is coming. By next summer, when plants are producing substances we can eat, we will probably not be alive. A sobering thought, but we have been living with that likelihood all along and have accepted its inevitability, as much as we can, and so we simply go on with our lives, staying mostly cheerful and keeping busy.

Philosophical point: none of us know when our lives will come to an end, or how the end will happen. But, stranded on this island, we recognize that the end is coming closer, if we are not rescued. So here's some advice to you: prepare for the inevitable, namely death. Make yourselves aware of the spiritual dimensions in life, the hope of eternal life. Don't dwell on dying, just spend a little of your precious time on earth looking beyond the here and now. I am sure that I am always in God's sight. And that faith not only makes death less frightening; it also makes life more precious and gives me purpose. As some poet put it long ago, "So live, that when thy summons comes to join that innumerable caravan where each shall take his chamber in the silent halls of death; thou go not like a quarry slave at night, scourged to his dungeon, but sustained and soothed by an unfaltering trust…." I probably have misquoted the poor guy, but I'm sure you get the idea. Be a good boy/girl scout about life and death: "Be prepared."

Donald G. Vedeler

And now, in a less morbid vein, remember that life is good, even when it may not be exactly what you want it to be. Take a moment, well, take many moments, to be thankful for the gift of life. Melanie, Harry, and I agree that just being alive is a good thing. We are contented, most of the time, with the adventure in which we find ourselves. So, when the sh-- hits the fan, make fertilizer? Enough of this nonsense!

Lay hold on life with <u>enthusiasm, optimism and faith</u>. If I said this while we were sitting in a warm living room by the fire, you might say, "easy for you to say." But in our present situation it is not as easy to say as it might be for you! Poor people living in remote and primitive areas have very little, but you often find them cheerful anyway.

It's getting dark, so I will end now.

Hugs and kisses to all of you.

Love, Grampa

Dear Grandchildren,

Today has been another gray day: sleet, freezing rain, and fog. Although we did have sunshine and some warmth a couple of days ago, maybe 40° at midday, today winds are blowing, and it's only in the teens.

But we still managed to enjoy our hike around the island, which we use to look for edible plants. We could not see more than ten feet as we walked, but that made each rock outcropping we came to more noticeable. And it dawned on us how beautiful and unique each one is! For the first time, after all these weeks, we felt like we were strolling through an art gallery! And then there was the coating of ice on the branches of bushes and grass. Absolutely beautiful! Imagining that you might someday read this, I want you to know what we experienced today.

We have been surrounded by this beauty: the rocks, the cliff, and the slope of the land. Although we have often appreciated the beauty of it, today was almost a religious experience walking in a wonderland of ice and fog. Just in case I don't survive this Island Adventure, I want you to know that we have moments of near ecstasy as we admire the beauty of nature here.

That's it for today's Robinson Crusoe information.

Open your eyes to the beauty in small things: a tree, bare branches against a winter sky, the song of a bird, a shaft of sunlight reaching down through a hole in the clouds, a smile from someone you pass, etc., etc., etc.

We just don't know what to do. We pray for guidance but are left with uncertainty. A message in that: God is not a magician at our beck and call. When and how and even if He answers prayer is up to Him, not us. So don't fuss at God just because you don't seem to receive an answer to your prayers. The three of us do find, however, that when we join hands and pray for guidance we feel inwardly better for having done so, answer or not. God listens. We may miss His response because we are looking for something other than what He has in mind. After all, He is God, you know! I guess maybe our eternal souls are in his care, but our physical existence is more up to us? There is a "great cloud of unknowing" around our human existence, after all is said and done. And maybe that is as it should be. We must live by faith, rather than with certainty. Faith is "the assurance of things hoped for, the conviction of things not seen."

But, I ramble. So I will close now, with love,

Grampa

Dear Grandkids,

Today it happened!!! The writing of this letter may be a waste of time! But I'll write it anyway, for posterity.

Today was bitter cold and breezy. We would guess the air temperature was in the 'teens, without the wind chill factored in, but with superb visibility. After lunch we braved the elements and took our walk, bundled up, old T-shirts wrapped around our noses and mouths, hands stuffed inside our pockets. Just another day in paradise, or so Melanie commented. But it was not "just another day!"

In the early afternoon I spotted a speck on the horizon. Another boat, I assumed. And it was. We watched it for twenty minutes and noticed it had grown slightly larger. With a minimum of hopefulness, we lit our signal fire again. We have done this maybe a dozen times, but to no avail.

By the time it was a roaring bonfire, and we had thrown large armloads of seaweed on it, the boat was recognizable as a boat. The huge cloud of smoke rose in the air and was blown back over the cliff behind us. But it was thick and should have been noticeable from out on the boat, if only someone was looking our way.

<u>The boat drew closer, until we could see figures on the deck. One figure stood on the bow waving his arms at us!</u> The boat drew to within a hundred yards of us, but could come no closer because of the heavy surf. The skipper turned the boat away from us, bow into the wind, and held the boat in position. We shouted and hollered. And we could see three figures shouting and hollering back. But we could hear nothing over the roar of the surf. Tears of joy ran down our cheeks, freezing in Harry's beard and mine.

After ten minutes of futile gesturing and shouting, it became apparent that this was the best we could hope for. A man emerged from the cockpit, pointed at the heavy surf, shrugged his shoulders, waved, and went back inside the cabin. White water appeared at the stern, and the boat began to move away.

We watched for an hour until the boat was no longer in sight.

I write this letter in the hope that a rescue will come soon, but also with a shadow of doubt lingering: did they think we might be willing explorers camped here intentionally?

Today's message: Don't be afraid to hope, but keep a realistic attitude. As they say, "Expect the worst, hope for the best, and take what comes."

We thought we should pack our gear, just in case. But what do we have to pack? Well, we have our letters and Melanie's food studies, and the list of the dead. Other than that we have ourselves, and the need to keep going as usual until we are rescued. It could be within days or a week. Or it could be never. We just don't know. So we toss a couple of peat globs on the fire, and life goes on.

I love you all so much. I hope and pray that this will be my last letter, for obvious reasons.

Love, Grampa

Dear Loved Ones,

It has been five days since we saw that boat, and we are caught in the middle of a fierce blizzard that struck the day after the boat left us. Shrieking winds, horizontal snowfall, and bitter cold temperatures. Drifts of snow have filled every space in the lee of rocks and ledges. We cannot leave the protection of our shelter for fear of being knocked down, or stumbling a few steps in the wrong direction and losing sight of the shelter. After all, it now has that white sail cover under the new snow. We stagger into the U-shaped firepit to relieve ourselves, for we dare not step out into the storm to accomplish that! Also we crawl out to add wood and peat globs to the fire.

And we pray.

We pray for strength not to lose heart. We pray that the storm will end. We pray for our deliverance, our survival. And amid the roar assaulting us from outside, we pray that our sturdy gully shelter can withstand the buffeting. We feel the whole structure tremble when especially strong gusts slam into it. As we nibble on the last of our smoked seagull, and open one of the few remaining cans (asparagus), we talk. Actually, we almost have to shout to be heard, even though we are sitting, and at other times reclining, within a few feet of each other.

We had been talking about miracles; in particular about miracles in which people were cured of terminal illnesses or major life threatening injuries were healed. We had also been talking about people who walked away from plane crashes, and about those who survived the World Trade Center attack on 9/11. Deep within, our souls are screaming for rescue.

We explored the knotty problem of those who died in any of the preceding scenarios, and those who walked away, thanking God for saving them. I wrote about this back in October, our 106th day here. So, I find myself back to the same topic, wondering if I should skip it this time. But I'm not going to skip it; as it is too important. How people think God acts in the world has been a stumbling block for many of my friends and parishioners. So I believe the matter bears repeating.

If we thank God that we escape death, while others with us in a situation of extreme danger did not escape, are we not being highly illogical. We feel grateful but does the theology behind that gratitude make sense? And might it not be a mental and spiritual trap later in life when life goes against us?

What about this: I survive a car wreck and you do not. Did God save me and, in effect, kill you? Suppose I lie in a hospital bed with a broken leg and a few gashes and say, "thank God I survived!" Do I also thank God that you died? Does God act in human moments and pluck some from death's door while letting others be destroyed? How does our belief that this is what happens show God's love? I cannot accept the "Oh, well, it's all part of God's Plan" concept.

I cannot believe that the great and loving God of all grants survival and death moment by moment and person by person.

When you believe God arbitrarily protects some and does not protect others, it becomes a logical matter to give up on God. I have known more people that I can count who have given up on church and given up on God. Among their reasons is the miracles issue. I know a former member of one of my army congregations whose wife was terribly injured in a car crash, blind and brain injured. He asked God to let her die in peace, but she lived on, and after many months he and his family finally decided to pull the plug. He asked me, "Where is God? Why didn't he let her go?" I had no answer. I never saw him again.

People have been told that God answers prayers. They have heard stories of miraculous cures and of people being saved from death and injury because they prayed for deliverance. So when their time of tribulation comes, they pray to God, asking for protection from harm. Yet the harm comes anyway. I know several army wives who came to the chapel to pray regularly that their husbands would survive their tour in Vietnam. When a husband came home unscathed, his wife praised God and asserted that God had protected her husband. But when another husband came home in a coffin, or with part of his head shot away and his power of speech gone, his wife cried, and asked me why God let this thing happen. And these wives stopped coming to chapel, because God no longer existed for them. One woman shot herself in the head a couple of days after confiding in me that God was a myth and prayer was pointless.

What a terrible shame that people who once believed in God turn their backs on their faith because of the mistaken notion that God will do miracles for them if they but ask sincerely. Would that I could have convinced them that God is spirit and that His workings are internal and everlasting, and that suffering, death, comfort, and life simply happen, that we should not ask for miracles and then be surprised when they don't occur.

So? We pray for rescue from this island. Our days are numbered, and we know this as we grow weaker, thinner, and run out of food. What if we are not rescued? Has God forsaken us? What if we are rescued? That would be wonderful, but what about others who have been stranded, prayed for rescue, and were not saved?

Are there survival miracles? Perhaps But maybe miracles happen within no matter what happens without. Are there great inner miracles when rescue does not happen? Is it miraculous when God does not rescue us physically from harm?

I leave you with this item of faith: Our best interests are best served by asking God for inner help: things like strength, wisdom, and assurance. That way, no matter what happens, we are with God and we are confident that we are always in his safekeeping. Miracles happen within, not without. "God is Spirit and they that worship Him must worship Him in spirit and in truth." There is a great, Eternal Truth in that affirmation, a Truth that transcends the physical. Remember, what is seen is temporal and temporary. What is unseen is Eternal.

Even though we three companions may die here, we are not forsaken, for we are with God now and always. We share that belief, deep down in our souls. So we face death with

Donald G. Vedeler

equanimity. Note that I didn't say we welcome it! We have discovered that we are not afraid to die, if that is to be our fate. Now that is a miracle!

If someday our bodies are found and our letters and notes are brought home to you, rejoice that we are with God, and that you will have these writings as memorials to three people who loved life, loved each other, and loved family and friends with all their hearts.

I love you. And yes, I am praying with all my heart that we will be found alive and returned to our loved ones. How or if we feel those prayers are answered depends in part on our view of what prayer's purpose is.

I see I am rambling again! So I will close for now, hoping that the beginning of the rest of our lives will be with you!

This has been a wonderful adventure together, and a terrible adventure together. We have sunk into the depths of despair and we have risen to the heights of joyous faith. All the letters I have written have come from the heart: the telling of our tale, the sharing of my beliefs and values, and the statements of my inexpressible love for each of you.

Love, Grampa

POSTSCRIPT

On Friday, December 8th, 2006, a thirty five foot fishing boat out of Alcan Harbor on Shemya Island, was on its way to its home port after an extended fishing and mail delivering expedition to Attu and Agattu Islands. One of the deckhands spotted what looked like a thin wisp of smoke rising from a small, uninhabited island far to the north. In his Near Island Russian-Aleut language, he pointed and called to the captain, "Is that smoke?"

The captain snatched up his binoculars and looked. "Yes, there is smoke!" he exclaimed.

"Do you think it's an eruption?" asked the crewmember.

The skipper shook his head, "I cannot tell. But, well, these are volcanic islands. I suppose it's possible. Might be some sort of lava vent or something. Let's go in and take a closer look." He spun the wheel and headed the vessel north.

A half hour later he raised his binoculars and looked again at the island several miles ahead. "It seems to be a fire of some sort. But, I don't think it's volcanic."

Twenty minutes passed. This time the captain shouted, "I think I see people! And up on the high ground some sort of bright colored thing." He scanned slightly to the left. "I see something white down in a low spot between the cliff on the right and the knob on the left."

Several hundred yards off the rocky shore, just beyond where heavy surf foamed and churned, he turned the boat into the wind and adjusted the engine to hold it in position. "I can't bring us any closer. I see three people!" He waved at the stranded people, and they waved back, jumping up and down. "I see their mouths moving, but the surf is overpowering the sound they might be making. We will have to leave them and go home. There we can go to the Americans at their airfield and tell them about this.

Seven days later, on Friday, December 15th, a U.S. Air Force helicopter from Eareckson Air Station on Shemya Island in the Rat Islands Group, landed on the island and rescued three Americans who claimed they had been stranded there for one hundred seventy days.

Author Gregg Sponney's Notes

We had high hopes that a rescue was on its way, even though the five day blizzard that arrived after the boat departed created grave doubts about our chances. Doubts about a rescue notwithstanding, we packed up the few belongings we wanted to have with us, especially our letters and notes, and stuffed them in Ferd Armstrong's seabag.

•

Back home, a week after our joyous Christmas family reunion, I shared my letters with my 38 year old son, Matt, whose home is six miles from ours. He and Susan read the first of them, with tears in their eyes and many exclamations of surprise. "Dad, this is an incredible story! The notes to Heidi and Ed and the rest of your grandchildren are beautiful!"

Sixteen year old Heidi added, "You know, Grampa, you should get this published. What an adventure and what advice to grandchildren everywhere!"

I hemmed and hawed for a bit. But I slowly came to realize that they were right: this story should be shared.

•

What you have read in the preceding pages, is a verbatim account of our adventure. I have left out the many scribbled out parts, and made a few grammatical and spelling corrections. And I did not, during those weeks, write down things that kept recurring, and all the various things we tried to eat, some of which gave us digestive problems of one sort or another. No need to go into details about that! Most of our days were spent as described: routinely. I never wrote down the hundreds of personal and private things the three of us shared about our past lives. The three of us probably know more about each other than our families do. My daughter, Beth Collins, who turned forty one last September, insisted that I leave the wording in its original form. She said that to edit the letters would be to rob them of their immediacy and spontaneity. I also note, as I read through the letters that I was often repetitious. When I suggested that I should get rid of some of the repeated ideas, Beth's husband, Ed, disagreed. "Keep the letters the way you wrote them," he insisted. So I offer my story with some apology for the often disjointed or disorganized format of the letters.

•

As I was preparing the manuscript for publication I came across something I had written back in 2001, long before our shipwreck. It's called "A Vision and a Prayer." I believe that it is important, and fits right in with the kinds of things I wrote in my letters, so I will include it here. All lives, all religions are in this life together.

A Vision and a Prayer

Sleep came slowly.

Far below, made tiny by distance, I saw, stretching from horizon to horizon, an expanse of homes, apartments, factories, stores, and office buildings. Green trees and bright grass filled spaces among the structures. Directly below me I saw a great circle of buildings. As I gravitated closer to the circle it became apparent that they all faced the center of a huge circular park, green with grass and pleasant brick walkways. At ground level the details of each building became more distinct. Swept along the street, I sailed rapidly around the circle watching the buildings speed by. They became mosques, temples, spired churches, and shrines of every type. Some were huge edifices of brick and stone, others smaller buildings of every size and shape; even tents and some, simply small open fields. Minarets, spires, and domes crowned many of these places of worship. Signs before each one identified them, many in languages I could not read. I knew in those moments that all the religious groups of the world were represented in this great round necklace of worship places.

Then, gently and subtly at first, came the sound. A whisper. At first I thought it might be leaves rustling in the breeze. Then it slowly became a murmur of blended human voices. Not strident or loud, but more like the gentle sound of friends gathered together. The voices drew my eyes to a wide thoroughfare that entered the circle. A distant multitude strolled closer filled the street from sidewalk to sidewalk. First their clothing became more distinct. Suits, robes, and garments of every color and type. And hair of many lengths, colors, and styles; heads, some topped with hats, turbans, and scarves. The faces emerged as brown, as white, as tan, and as yellow. Men, women, and children walked together. Wheelchairs and stretchers mingled among the races of the world as they spilled into the round park. Friends parted from friends as groups made their way to different places of worship. The huge throng continued to flood through the circle and into the buildings. After what seemed like a long time, the park was empty and silent. A bright light increased gradually, filling the view until everything had become a pure, peaceful, glowing whiteness.

I gradually awoke, my entire being encompassed by an overwhelming and comforting sense of peace.

A Prayer

Open my mind to see beyond my private walls.
Free my spirit to soar above my valley.
Gentle my heart to hold the world.

Enable my dreams to reach
    for a vision of all humanity
    walking up the Hill of the Lord,
    together.

●

The reader may be interested to know a bit about our island. It is located among the Near Islands of the Aleutian Island chain. They are called the Near Islands because they are far to the west of Alaska, near Russia. I don't recall what the island was called, if I ever knew. The experience of being rescued, deloused, brought back to health and returned home, completely overshadows any recollection of the name of that little island in the cold sea.

We estimated that our island was about three quarters of a mile long, east to west, and maybe one thousand seven hundred feet wide. The cliff to the east, where we displayed the brightly colored spinnaker sail, was perhaps a hundred feet high. Many rocks surrounded the island, creating a barrier to boats and a spectacular venue for the explosions and surges of waves. On the north northeast side there are several sandy beaches. It was high up adjacent to those beaches that we found the grain. Also, you may recall that on our twentieth we had an exciting "fish experience" when the gulls called our attention to the hundreds of fish in the waves. The fish, I was told while on Shemya Island, were capelins, and for about a week in July of each year they swim up sandy beaches during a high tide and deposit eggs, then wriggle back into the water and depart. The seagulls swarm the areas for the food fest, and it was their raucous noise and swooping behavior that drew our attention to the strange event. Capelin were consumed raw, or cooked, or smoked and dried by early natives of the Aleutian Islands.

The weather is lousy, to put it plainly. The average yearly temperature in that area is 38°. In the summer, the average is around 60°. As you may have surmised from reading the book, fog and rain are very common. There are normally about two hundred and fifty rainy days per year! Because of this, our clothes and bedding were damp most of the time, which made for constant misery. We were quite fortunate to have unusually warm temperatures and less rain than usual!

Those ferocious winds that twice destroyed our lean-to in those first days on the island are common in the Aleutians. They are called willawas, and over the years frequently did major damage to structures, caused plans to crash, and ships to flounder.

Had we still been there in January we would have experienced average temperatures below 30° with wind chills below zero! Would we have survived? Who knows? Personally, I think we would have died of malnutrition and the sustained impact of the bitter cold and dampness on our weakened bodies. We are glad we were rescued before then!

We learned more about the Aleutian Islands, especially the Rat Islands and the Near Islands, from our Air Force friends on Shemya Island during our three day stay with them. The medical personnel provided excellent care, and the cooks put out extra effort to make the food tasty. A couple of enlisted friends confided in us that the diet on these remote bases was usually repetitive and bland. I was in the military long enough to know that out-of-the-way bases did not enjoy a wide variety of buffet type dining facilities. The cooks at those remote duty stations did the best they could with the facilities and food stuffs they had. What they served while we were there seemed like a sumptuous feast to the three of us!

I wish there was some way to transport each of you readers to "our island." Then you could see it for yourself, and get a truer sense of what those one hundred seventy days meant to Harry O'Toole, Melanie Pickett, and me.

●

To Harry and Melanie: my deepest thanks for helping me survive, both mentally and physically. Alone, I would surely have perished. My prayers are with you. May your health and happiness, like mine, be a source of joy beyond words. Although we are now separated by many miles, it is always good to receive your emails and occasionally talk with you on the phone. By the time this book is in print, Melanie, Harry, and I will have gathered together, with as many family members as can make it, on December 11th, 2007 for a Celebration of Thanksgiving.

To my grandchildren and the many other grandchildren, who I hope will read this story: may what I have written in some small way help each of you to find your own brand of wisdom, faith, health, love, and happiness!

Gregg Sponney
U.S.Army Chaplain, retired
April 20, 2007

AUTHOR DONALD VEDELER'S NOTES

About the Book

This book began, years ago, as a book of combined elements: devotions, religious philosophy, and sermons. About a year ago, I emailed my friend Janice Rand Tucker, a college and high school classmate, (author of *The Sun Still Shines: Living with Chronic Illness*) about the book I was writing. She asked, "What do you hope to accomplish by writing this book?" My answer was simple: I wanted to share some personal beliefs that have become important to me over the years, with the hope that people who read them would think about them and let them affect their lives, hopefully for the better. A friend in Florida asked, "Who do you think will read it?" Well, that stumped me! Who would pick up my book? Would there be any audience, or market, at all for an unknown religious writer's book? Janice's husband, Tom, a retired minister, suggested, "How about letters from a grandfather to his grandchild?" And I asked myself: why not have the grandfather write to all of his grandchildren, not just one grandchild?

These helpful questions sparked my enthusiasm, gave direction to my efforts, and led me into more questions. Why would a grandfather write to his grandchildren? Wouldn't he rather talk with them in person? What situation might he find himself in, such that he would, in a sense, be "forced" to write the letters? What if "Grampa Gregg" became stranded on an uninhabited island? I ruled out a tropical island, imagining that survival would be too easy, provided there was drinkable water. "What about the Aleutian Islands?" I asked myself. After finding out more about them, I was convinced that area was the best and most challenging setting for the story. The more research I did into the western Aleutian Islands, the more intriguing a survival story set there appeared. In my imagination I could feel the three survivors' mounting worry that they would never be rescued, even as they hoped, and prayed, that they would. And a book was born!

I live in Florida among many grandparents. Some are close to their grandchildren and see them frequently. Others rarely see them. A common regret among us is the very few occasions in which we have had any serious talks with our grandchildren. For the most part, when we are

121

around our grandchildren, we talk with them about school (grade school, high school, college) or their activities, friends and jobs. Seldom do we chat with them about what we believe is important in life. Time and life move on and we discover that we have missed the opportunities to talk with them about their inner lives, their doubts and beliefs, their hopes and fears. This novel emerged, in part, from that regret. The book is a final chance to share personal motives and beliefs with our beloved grandchildren, whatever their ages.

I envisioned *A SHIPWRECK SURVIVOR'S TALE Letters to His Grandchildren* as a book of practical religious and moral affirmations embedded in an exciting tale of survival.

●

Should you want a way to go back to certain ideas, here is an alphabetical list of 45 "serious topics" by DAY #.

a Universal God and faith groups 122

anger at God 9

care for your body 25

courage in adversity 42

decisions & choices 84

eternity, faith & salvation 133

faith, evil & love 106

gambling, risk taking, values 69

God, our private magician? 153

good grief 8

happiness: a by-product not a goal 118

how we become religious 36

joy out of despair 93

lust for power; the power trap 62

money, stewardship 88

optimism, love & a brighter world 22

openness, self-sharing 120

please and thank you 35

prepare - God's care & keeping 149

Psalm 23 58

saviorS or savior? 63

smoking 77

strength within you 86

when things look bad… 54

anger & hurt feelings 13

appreciate beauty! 153

choices, ISness of the WAS 74

death and life beyond death 55

Does God micromanage? 112

expect the unexpected 33

follow your dream 72

giving up on God 168

Golden Rule, the 66

good in people19

hope & realistic expectations 163

humor in life 53

love of self, love of neighbor 91

miracle of the loaves & fishes 142

never give up hope 44, 89

original sin, evil & goodness 45

people are precious, be gentle 23, 34

power of positive thinking 46

profanity… God's name in vain 81

rescue & love 136

sharing your private self 120

spirit world, the 59

take nothing for granted - open mind 29

Historical Notes

Before dawn on June 7th, 1942, under the command of Rear Admiral Sentaro Omari, 2,500 men of The Imperial Northern Force of the Japanese army swarmed ashore on Kiska and Attu Islands of the westernmost islands of the Aleutians.

Over the next few weeks they consolidated their hold on neighboring islands, building numerous observation and defensive bunkers. This explains the presence of old, World War II, bunkers on many of the islands. I toyed with having my three castaways find an old Japanese bunker up on the east end of that cliff, but that would have made things too easy for them!

The Japanese high command anticipated that Allied bombing and even a likely invasion of Japan would be launched by way of the Western Aleutians. Their invasion of the Near Islands was their preemptive move designed to end that threat. An excellent account of all this is found in *The Thousand Mile War: World War II in Alaska and the Aleutian Islands*, by Brian Garfield, [New York, 1969], a fascinating, nonfiction book about a relatively unknown part of World War II in the Pacific.

●

Sometime after May of 1943, United States forces built a giant 10,000 foot concrete runway on Shemya Island. By 1969 the giant B29 hanger and huge hospital were crumbling into ruin. But things changed. American military personnel reestablished a base on Shemya Island. On 9 April 1993 Shemya Air Force Base was renamed Eareckson Air Station in a ceremony held later on 19 May 1993. The 11th Air Force Association renamed the base in honor of Colonel William O. Eareckson who, from 1941 to 1943 personally led missions against the Japanese forces on Kiska and Attu.

●

If you have enjoyed this book, please:
Ask your local library to purchase a copy. Share your copy with someone. Write, e-mail or phone relatives and friends and tell them about the book. Order copies from any local or on-line bookseller, such as Barnes & Noble: (bn.com) – Booksamillion.com – iUniverse.com – Amazon.com, and give them as gifts. Purchase my earlier two novels in THE CHAPLAINS Adventure Series: *Moles in the Eagle's Nest*, and *Tainted Hero*. Write to me at 20670 Persimmon Pl., Estero, FL 33928. Or look me up in the on-line white pages and call, and perhaps go online to Barnes & Noble and write a brief comment – about any of my books.

●

Donald G. Vedeler

These two basic needs mentioned on DAY 138 (for love and for rescue) are primary forces in the lives of the protagonists of my three chaplain adventure novels.

Love your neighbor as yourself. Love God. Make the world a better place for your having been in it. Follow your dream!

September 2009
Donald Vedeler
U. S. Army Chaplain (retired)
Estero, Florida